BEYOND THE DARKNESS

By
S. J. BYRNE

ARMCHAIR FICTION
PO Box 4369, Medford, Oregon 97504

*For more information about Armchair Books and products, visit our
website at…*

www.armchairfiction.com

Or email us at…

armchairfiction@yahoo.com

TO PROBE THE MYSTERY OF THE BLACK ABYSS MEANT DEATH!

His name was Nad and the only world he had ever known was a few square kilometers in area. He and his fellow Passengers had all the food they could eat and there was always comfortable shelter to be had. Mating was allowed, to a certain degree, and there were numerous forms of entertainment available to stave off boredom. Yes, he and the other Passengers were well taken care of by the Navigators—so long as one did not question what lay outside the Door or its darkness beyond. The Door was a thing to be feared and occasionally the Navigators sent people through that door and into the black abyss beyond—people who were deemed undesirable or whose minds had become too inquisitive. But Nad was perpetually restless, for he and his fellow Passengers had no knowledge of man's past. There was no human history to delve into, no course of events that explained the existence of their small, pitiful world. Then one day Nad dared to raise a questioning voice, and soon he was thrown into a bizarre chain of events that threatened not only his own life, but the existence of the entire human race as he knew it…

FOR A COMPLETE SECOND NOVEL, TURN TO PAGE 107

CAST OF CHARACTERS

NAD

He wanted answers to the uncertainties about the world within which he lived; but to ask the questions might cost him his life.

LYLWANI

Strong and loyal, her love of Nad knew no bounds; in this her mind was set. But one could always have their mind…changed.

SARGON

On the surface he just seemed like a typical despotic thug, but what was the real secret he hid from the people of his world?

YIDDIR

His reputation as a great leader and a brilliant scientist was a well-guarded secret that could cost him his life if exposed.

RON

He was essentially the runt of the litter, with a club foot and a streak of faintheartedness that was nearly unparalleled.

YLDRA

She loved Ron with all her heart; but it was hard being in love with someone who was a complete and utter coward.

KRYLORNO

He thought of himself as a poet and an idealist, but in truth he was little more than a jealous fool.

CHAPTER ONE

LYLWANI'S slender, pink hands clutched Nad's arm.

"Do we have to look?" she said rather than asked.

Nad's bushy, blond brows only lowered over his gray eyes and his mouth tightened into a scowl of hate and defiance as he watched the execution.

"Those are orders," he said. "Orders! Always orders. Disobey or even question an order and you get what he's going to get..."

Nad's red-headed younger brother, Ron, nervously shifted the almost negligible weight of his frail body from his club foot to his good one and drew in closer to Nad.

"Be careful!" he hissed. "You'll be overheard!"

His round, blue eyes surveyed the faces of the hundred or so Passengers gathered there, and his female companion, holding his hand, felt in it the reflection of his terror. Yldra, she of the long blue hair and the pale white skin, had lost her customary smile, and her great, dark eyes glistened on the verge of tears.

"Poor Gradon!" she said to Ron. "He was so good and kind. Now he goes to the Abyss..."

A frightened murmur arose from the crowd of Passengers as *the Door* slid soundlessly aside, exposing them momentarily to the execution chamber that would soon open into the Abyss. Sargon M-I3-NT, Navigator, shoved old Gradon unceremoniously into the large chamber, and *the Door* closed upon him forever.

Through its crystal clear substance they could see Gradon plainly. He turned his back on the dark destruction that approached him and faced all his old friends, a weary smile on his kindly face. As Sargon reached for the control valve, Gradon waved goodbye not only to those present but to those other thousands of Passengers who had been ordered to witness his execution in the visiplates.

Then the valve turned, and the Passengers hid their faces.

But Sargon shouted at them.

"Look! As you persist in seeking the answers to the Unknown, so shall you be sent *into* it—into the Abyss, from which there is no return! Thus the discontented and the trouble-makers shall die! *Look,* I said!"

And the squad of Navigators with him sprayed the Passengers with pain ray until they looked.

By the time Nad's party looked up, there was nothing much left to see. A frozen splatter of blood on the outer surface of *the Door,* and beyond—mystery of mysteries, especially to Nad—was the gaping opening into the Abyss.

Out there was gray-black nothingness. Why? What was it? Was it only another type of wall, a wall of endlessness beyond impenetrable walls of metal? Walls of cryosite, resistant to the terrific blows of meteors form the Abyss. Walls of emptiness and the Unknown. Walls of the mind. Seek not! Know not! Obey and be content—or die like Gradon, one of the finest men Nad had ever known.

As some of Gradon's closest friends cried aloud in their bereavement, the outer door to the Abyss closed, and Sargon and his men moved toward Nad's group. Nad knew this was not without premeditation, for Sargon had evidenced a marked interest in Lylwani for some time.

As Lylwani stepped close to Nad, and Ron and Yldra stepped deferentially aside to make way for Sargon, Nad's lifelong frustration and indignation burst their bonds. He stepped in front of Sargon and deliberately blocked his path.

Nad was tall, lean, tense and white. His gray eyes met Sargon's black stare unwaveringly. Sargon was slightly taller, broader of shoulder, and thicker in the limbs and neck. His reddish complexion deepened visibly in sudden rage, and his thick, leonine mane of jet-black hair seemed to bristle.

"Well, idiot!" he snapped. "Step aside. Haven't you learned your lesson yet?"

"Yes," replied Nad, in a strangely subdued tone of voice. "I have learned my lesson. You have *all* the advantages and we have none. I only intend to make a constructive suggestion, with your permission."

Ron whimpered in his fright and tugged at his brother's arm, but Nad waved him back, impatiently.

"It had better be constructive," warned Sargon. "Speak, man. We haven't got all day."

One of the other Passengers, an old, gray-haired man with pale blue eyes and a leathery skin, crowded close to listen as Nad spoke.

"The occasional trouble you experience with us Passengers would be eliminated," Nad said, "if you simply gave us more information. For instance—"

"Information!" shouted Sargon. "There *is* no information. This is the world in which you were born, and here you will live and die. Why must you grow discontented when you are adequately supplied with food, clothing and shelter and entertainment without having to work for it? Here there are only seven thousand of you, with kilometers of spacious room in which to live and play. Yet you complain! You do not trust the Navigators upon whom your life and welfare depends. It is because of this ungratefulness on your part that we have lost patience with you, and these disciplinary measures will continue to be taken until you accept the advantages with which you have been provided. What *more* do you want?"

"Sargon," said Nad, unmoved by this tirade, "do you know your own father?"

"Of course, stupid! I—" Then Sargon bit his lip and he reddened visibly. He had been tricked into an admission he would not have made otherwise.

"You see, that's the difference between the Navigators and the Passengers," said Nad, rapidly. "We don't know who our parents were, and parents can't recognize their own children. The only reason I call Ron-E-251-P my brother is because you have told me he is my brother, and that was perhaps unintentional on your part. You Navigators have memory. You have deprived us of that so that we will forget. Forget *what*, Sargon? What is it you Navigators are so afraid that we will remember?"

Sargon's big fists clenched. "Shut up," he blurted out. "Do you want what Gradon got?"

Nad heard other Passengers gasp in alarm. Lylwani called out his name pleadingly and Ron ran away, taking Yldra with him. But the old man with the pale blue eyes drew even closer as he watched Nad.

As Sargon advanced slowly upon him and Nad slowly gave way before him, the latter continued. Now that he had started he could not stop himself.

"Our language is filled with strange words that we use without realizing their full significance," he said rapidly. "Why do you say 'day' or 'night' or 'month' or 'year'? What is the true meaning of these strange divisions of time where time never varies? You say that here there are only seven thousand Passengers. Are there more elsewhere? What *is* a Passenger, actually, other than a man or a woman who is not a Navigator and who is forbidden to enter section N or M? Why is it such an advantage not to have to work? Did Passengers work before? At what—and where? These walls that separate us from the Abyss were made by men. What was here before men knew enough to make them? Why are we three distinct types of people? There are the pale, blue-haired ones, such as Yldra V-57-P, and there is a second kind, like myself and my brother, who have the letter E attached to our names. Then there is the third type, like Lylwani here, with a pinkish complexion and jet-black hair like yours. You are Sargon M-I3-NT and she is called Lylwani M-78I-P. Your kind has the letter M attached to all your names. You say this is our natural world in which we have been born, yet you have also mentioned the 'growing problem' of inbreeding. I have heard the Navigator medicos remark that my brother's club foot is the result of the problem. I can only conclude that our present state is not a natural one, but rather—"

At that moment, Sargon struck Nad with all his might and he went down hard on the metal floor with blood spurting from his lower lip. Lylwani dropped instantly beside him.

"I let you talk," said Sargon, "so that you would incriminate yourself completely. You will be executed, of course."

"Why?" cried Lylwani, rising quickly to her feet and facing him. "His crime is only recognizable in relation to arbitrary opinion on your part. What good will it do to destroy him, too? A thousand more will ask the same questions!"

Sargon's thick lips curled in amusement as he surveyed the lithe young woman before him, but secretly he admired again, as he had so often in the past, her long, raven-black hair lying across her shapely, pink shoulders; and he hungered for her full, young lips while he thrilled at the fiery spirit that stared at him out of her dark green eyes.

"Don't get yourself in trouble, too, beautiful," he said. "Take him away and get out of my sight, both of you!"

"But will he be executed?" Lylwani persisted, as Nad rose slowly to his feet.

Sargon raised his thick brows as though surprised by the question. "Naturally!" he said. And then he walked away with his men.

"Oh Nad! Nad!" cried Lylwani, throwing her arms around his neck. "I couldn't live without you! They can't kill you! They can't!"

Nad was apparently oblivious to all this. He did not feel the many sympathetic hands that touched him or hear the voices of the Passengers as they crowded thickly about him. His gray eyes only stared at Sargon's receding back.

"If anything will preserve me," he said, wiping more blood from his lip, "it will be hate—and the will to live until my hands have closed around Sargon's fat neck. They won't be able to take me until I have done at least that!"

IN THE high arching tube ramp that crossed above the great Recreation Center, Ron and Yldra hurried toward their own section, where they knew at least Lylwani would eventually return. A quarter kilometer below them, through the transparent metal floor of the tube, they could see over a thousand Passengers returning listlessly to their amusements, some bathing in giant pools of chemically treated water, others playing games or working out on exercise machines. Some Passengers flew transparent globes in changing formations far above the floor, engaging in an aerial game called three-dimensional chess. All around the gigantic chamber were countless observation tiers and refreshment mezzanines, where observers looked down at the activities below or watched the aerial chess game. Ron and Yldra had seen all this for as long as they could remember. It was their unchanging world, without beginning or end.

In the middle of the ramp they were suddenly confronted by Krylorno, the poet, whose well-known poems had so often alluded openly to Yldra. Tall, lean, dark of complexion and extremely aquiline of feature, he deliberately blocked Ron's path, fixing his hypnotic eyes upon him. Behind him crowded a group of almost a hundred other Passengers, many of whom were relatively close acquaintances of both Yldra and Ron. They were of the younger set, mostly, and appeared to be emotionally geared to the strange fanaticism that lighted the face of Krylorno.

Krylorno, the silver-tongued, sneered at Ron. "Well, Club Foot, we saw your cowardly performance in the visiplates. Why did you desert your brother in the most heroic moment of his life? If he was moved to confront his tormentors at last, why did you not stand firm beside him instead of slithering away in the torrent of your fears? Can you name any valid reason for prolonging your meaningless existence? For what is left but the validity of heroism? Of what use is a groveling coward?"

Ron's thin face paled and he seemed to be on the verge of tears, but Yldra defended him.

"Have you not heard of instinct?" she said, in the soft, benevolent tones that were the reflection of her well-beloved personality. She smiled sadly as she continued. "Whatever life may be, we all have an instinct to cling to it, and in times of stress and terror this instinct of self-preservation is like a mother that defends its child against reason. Ron is not alone. I am confused as he is, and so, I am sure, are the rest of you. So give us peace and let us pass."

"Wait…" persisted Krylorno, addressing her. "Why you care for this coward I cannot imagine, but if you do, then perhaps you would prefer to have him embrace the greatest advantage life can offer."

"And that is?"

"The single reality of *death,*" he answered, solemnly.

Ron stared at Krylorno and trembled. Yldra's wondering gaze wandered from Krylorno's enigmatic face to the fanatic faces of his followers. Then she sought his eyes again.

"I do not understand," she said.

Krylorno laughed. Suddenly, as he answered her, his voice deepened and seemed to fill the ramp tube.

"Oh Darkness that is Light!" he chanted.

"Oh mighty Judge that offers peace forever in abysmal night!

"Oh Truth that gives me naked Nothing for falsely vested life.

"Where in an instant that is ever I may be free of Wrong or Right!"

He glared now at Ron and his voice crescendoed.

"Oh take me from this putrid shell. This delusion-veined mirror of life's hell.

"And swallow up the atoms of my being in the freedom of oblivion.

"Beyond this dungeon cell!"

He grasped Ron's white tunic and pulled him close. "Do you understand me?" he asked.

"No!" Ron cried out. "You are insane. Let me go!"

"Krylorno!" Yldra exclaimed, separating the two. "Whatever are you driving at?"

Krylorno waved his hand at his followers. "We are all of the same opinion," he answered. "Life is meaningless. We prefer death. It is the only truth we can conceive of. It is release from all torment and frustration. Why not join us?"

"You mean—mass suicide?" Yldra blanched swiftly and looked at her friends in alarm.

"Yes," Krylorno triumphed. "Why not? It's painless in the disposal tubes. You enter the dumping locks, a valve is turned, and your worries are over. You explode out into the Abyss like Gradon did. There's nothing to it…"

Yldra's eyes glistened in her consternation. "But that's hideous. It's—it's rank insanity!"

"No!" exclaimed Krylorno. "It is ultimate intelligence. Do you think this empty farce of life without memory freedom or reason is worth clinging to? Only in the clarity of approaching death can we appreciate the magnificence of our decision to die. In a few hours we will be one with the Abyss, so leave this limping coward to cling to his rag of an existence and join us in the glory of oblivion…"

At that moment, the sonophone beneath a nearby visiplate rasped into life, and a strange voice addressed specifically those who were gathered at that one location on the tube ramp. The voice was strange because it was obviously not that of a Navigator. All the Passengers had been trained throughout their lives to recognize the arrogant, dictatorial tones of the Navigators. This voice was kind, patient—even fatherly. Moreover, it activated only the single sonophone in their vicinity, leaving the visiplate blank, which was an unprecedented occurrence.

"Man has a magnificent purpose to accomplish in the living flesh," the voice said. *"We should be willing to accept death only when we have contributed all we can toward the accomplishment of that purpose. This purpose has been hidden from you by the Navigators who have robbed you of memory so that you would not revolt. It cannot be explained to you until you have been informed of many more facts for which there is no time at present… But there is a purpose that you will only defeat by seeking death prematurely. You must be patient and cling to your lives as your most precious possession—until the time of liberation arrives…"*

All present were too astonished to speak, except Krylorno. He stepped in front of the blank visiplate and said, "Who speaks to us of liberation without showing his face?"

Immediately, the two-way sonophone replied, *"Your, question must remain unanswered until the time comes. And if you truly seek an answer to your existence, if you wish for a real reason for living, and if you are desirous of a true, constructive change in your status of life, then tell no Navigator you have heard my voice—because otherwise they might subject you to the M-Ray again."*

"What is the M-Ray?" asked Krylorno.

"It is that which they have used against you to rob you of memory. I can say no more, but I will contact you and certain other Passengers again. In the meantime, you may refer to me among yourselves as—X."

There ensued a long moment of silence, after which Yldra found her voice and said, "Then it is as Nad suspected all along."

"What do you mean?" Krylorno asked her, staring at her intently.

"The Navigators are withholding knowledge from all of us. There is some greater meaning to all this other than just living and eating and sleeping and trying endlessly to amuse ourselves with senseless games." Her dark eyes were wide with excitement. She turned to Ron and grasped his hand. "Let's see if we can find Nad," she said. "We must tell him of this message. And you..." She stopped to look back at Krylorno. "...use that persuasive tongue of yours to keep us all together and alive. Do you think the Navigators would care if you committed mass suicide? They are only looking for excuses to reduce our numbers. Did you ever think that there are only a few hundred of them against thousands of us?"

For once, Krylorno was at a loss for words. But Yldra's friends and the others who had followed Krylorno raised a cheer for her.

"She's right!" they cried. "And so is X."

"Yldra," said Ron, as he limped along beside her. "You are beautiful and intelligent. Why do you care for me?"

Yldra looked at him curiously. "Don't ask me to explain that, Ron," she answered. "There is no explanation, except that—well, we've been together since as far back as I can remember. I—I don't know any other way of life."

"I love you, Yldra."

"You're sweet."

"I'm a worthless coward."

"You only imagine that you are. Come on! We've got to find Lylwani—and Nad, if he has not been arrested already…"

CHAPTER TWO

NAD and Ron, like all other single, adult, male Passengers, shared quarters with several other men. Each unit of this type consisted of ten private rooms with a common bath. Meals were taken in large mess rooms serving a hundred such units, so no unit could boast of its own dining room. However, common to each unit was a small reception and recreation room where friends of both sexes could be entertained.

Yldra and Lylwani lived in a similar unit shared by single women. If a man and woman desired each other as mates, they found it necessary to adhere to a strict rule of the Navigators. They would apply to the authorities for permission to live together, and once this was granted there was seldom any permission given to separate again, chiefly because of the nature of the marriage process. Marriage was officially recognized when a pair authorized to live together produced a child, at which time they were considered to be bound together for life. Cohabitation was permitted for an indefinite period without children, and couples who had not reproduced were permitted to separate upon proper application to the authorities, although such a circumstance was rare. Only if they reproduced were they considered to be married and inseparable, however. Promiscuity was not permitted, entirely on the basis of practical rather than moral reasons.

It was in the recreation room of Nad's unit where Nad, Ron, Lylwani, and Yldra contacted each other again, and Yldra told Nad about the mysterious voice. She had to speak in a very low tone because of the ever present sonophones. It would be practically suicidal, she knew, for them to let such talk be intercepted by the Navigators. Ron, as usual, was worried. He tried to take Yldra out of the room in case the Navigators suddenly decided to investigate.

But Nad detained him. "Not this time, Ron," he said, grimly. There was a new, intense expression on his face. "We're all in this together. Whatever it is we're going to do we'll do together or die in the attempt! You'll stick with us now, every step…"

"But Nad!" Ron protested. "If we are arrested we'll not be able to do anything. Besides, what *can* we do even if we are not arrested for all this mysterious talk, or even if you are not executed as Sargon says you will be? What is our purpose or plan? What's it all about?"

"That's what I'm going to find out," Nad replied. "I've got to find this 'X' person and work with him. If the price is my life or your lives, it's worth it."

"No!" protested Ron.

"Yes!" said Lylwani and Yldra in unison.

And Lylwani added, "You're right, Nad. There is no purpose in mere existence here unless we can unravel the whole mystery and see where we are going."

Nad had been lost in thought, momentarily, but now he looked up suddenly at Lylwani, his eyes wide in astonishment. "What did you say?" he demanded rather than asked.

"I said we've got to clear up this whole mystery and—and—"

"And *what!*" He glared at her, a triumphant smile on his lips.

"And—see—where we are going…"

"Exactly!" he exclaimed, smacking the palm of his hand with his fist. *'We're going somewhere!* We're on a journey! This metal-walled world of ours is like one of the flying globes used for the aerial chess games in the Recreation Hall. It is moving *through* the Abyss. The Navigators have erased our memory of where we really came from!"

He paced rapidly back and forth in front of his astounded little audience. "That means there was another life on the *outside,* at the beginning of the Abyss somewhere. And maybe—maybe there is a new life, after we *cross* the Abyss. Or maybe—" He paused, staring into nothingness.

"Maybe what, Nad?" Lylwani asked, excitedly.

"Maybe the Navigators are lost and won't admit it…"

AT that moment, without warning, two Navigators stepped into the room. It was too late for anyone to do anything. The Navigators, young and arrogant in their esoteric knowledge, immediately approached Nad and seized him.

"Come along," said one of them. "Sargon's orders."

In a wholly unexpected move Nad broke their grips on him and ran for the corridor. Both Navigators fired Stun Rays after him but he was shielded by the metal walls just in time.

Much to the surprise of Nad's friends remaining in the reception room, the two young guards only grinned at each other and shrugged. One of them reached over to the wall and unlocked a small compartment with a master key. Inside the compartment was a switch that tied the sonophone in the room to all the others in the system. Once the switch was thrown, the operator had at his disposal a universal public address system.

"Alert! Alert!" he called into the instrument. "All guards! Capture escaped Passenger condemned to execution, Nad E-250-P, last seen in Q sector, deck fifteen. He is unarmed. When captured, bring prisoner to H. Q. That is all."

The guard who had made the announcement locked up the converter switch box and turned to his companion.

"Is that guy crazy?" he asked. "How does he figure he has a chance?"

When they had left the room, Ron was near to fainting in his terror. "You see? You see?" he said hysterically. "Now he's got us all into trouble!"

Lylwani had a faraway look in her eyes. Silently, she left the room. Ron stood there trembling in his helplessness, for even if he had possessed courage, he lacked the knowledge of what to do. Yldra covered her face and began to cry…

LYLWANI presented herself to the astonished guard and said simply, "I have come to see Sargon." She gave him her name.

While she waited outside the great cryosite door, she could not suppress a feeling of terror. She had asked permission to enter section N, forbidden heretofore to all Passengers except women taken in as the chosen mates of the Navigators. Strange and terrifying were the imagined tales she had heard concerning this place, which was the citadel of the Navigators. Childlike in her ignorance she half believed she would never emerge from the place once she entered it. But her purpose was fixed unshakably in her mind. What she was doing was the only solution she could conceive of—for Nad. She was sure that the mysterious person known as X held the answer to all their problems, and if Nad could be free to join forces with X one day, it would be far more important than her own personal destiny.

The guard returned with a second Navigator, who led her to Sargon, Chief of the Navigator guards. So confused was her perception due to her increasing misgivings, that she failed to notice anything unusual about the about the shining corridors through which she was taken, until she was admitted to Sargon's own office.

This was not at all like the Passenger type living quarters or reception rooms. It was unusually spacious and comfortable, as though it had been designed for an officer of much higher rank than that of Sargon. On the floor was a soft, furry substance that felt luxurious under her thin sandals as she walked across it. Its strange, soft fibers were of purest white and she could not imagine of what it was composed. Even Sargon's desk was of an alien substance—pure black, but like glass and scintillating with lights inherent within itself. On the walls were curious pictures that she could not understand at all. Among them was a very unintelligible one under glass, and beneath it was a metal plate bearing the meaningless title: *Nebula in Andromeda...*

Sargon sat inscrutably at his desk, but he motioned her to a large cushioned chair beside him. It was such a chair as Lylwani had never sat in before—soft and caressing, seeming to cradle her whole body like a cloud.

"Why have you come here?" he asked. "Is it because of Nad? His career is just about at an end, you know." He watched her intently.

Lylwani sat up wide-eyed. "Then they *did* capture him?" she said.

Sargon's brows lowered to emphasize a penetrating gaze. "What *else* could happen?" he asked.

Lylwani lowered her head to hide her face, and her long, dark hair fell across her shoulders, but Sargon noticed that they trembled. He rose to his feet and stood looking down at her.

"You have come to request leniency for him," he told her. "What would you offer in return?"

Lylwani looked up at him, suddenly struggling for self-composure. "You want me," she said, tonelessly. "Give him freedom and I will bear you child." In the language of the Passengers there was no actual word for marriage.

A light leaped into Sargon's eyes but was gone almost in the same instant. "A Navigator's woman remains forever within section N," he replied. "You would have to be content never to see Nad again."

By now Lylwani's face had lost its natural, pinkish complexion. It was white. And her voice was like that of an automaton as she spoke.

"Let me see him free, and I will be your woman," she said.

Sargon chuckled. "What makes you think I would not take you anyway?" he asked. "I have planned it this way for a long time."

Lylwani's eyes widened. "But that is against Navigator law!" she protested. "Not even a Passenger woman may be forced—"

"Forget it," Sargon interrupted. "There are many things you don't know—too many things. Startling and amazing things, Lylwani. Things that would enable you to understand why we Navigators are doing what the Passengers believe to be unreasonable, even though we do it for their own protection. I have wanted to share this knowledge with you, as well as certain personal triumphs, but that will only be possible when you have became my mate. I promise you I will do all I can for Nad—if you promise to stay here now and be content never to return to the Passengers."

For answer, Lylwani buried her head in the gas-foam cushions of her chair and cried uncontrollably. But for Sargon it was answer enough...

WHEN Nad ran from his own quarters to escape the Navigator guards, he had in mind a certain destination known as V sector, where there were whole batteries of living units unassigned. Vaguely, he tried to formulate some plan of action as he ran, but he could not yet see his way clear beyond the mere possibility of hiding out for a very brief period in V sector.

Passengers in the corridors instantly made way for him as he ran, in spite of the warning cry of the Navigator guard over the sonophones. There was a sickly expression of incomprehension on most of their faces. They could not understand resistance or flight. Why resist or flee? Where could one go? It was easier to give up. Surrender to the Navigators if they want you. Death was a certainty. Life, at its best, was a monotonous, meaningless effort.

But Nad ran for his life, and he felt that he was running, too, for *all* their lives. This hopeful premonition gave him a new strength, courage and determination such as he had never known before. Something seemed to whisper: *Now! The time has arrived! Make a break for it!*

On deck eighteen, near V sector, the Navigators began to close in on him. Panting loudly, he ran down a passage and suddenly ducked into a deserted room. With narrowed eyes glaring like those of a wild animal at bay, he thought rapidly and with a new clarity and confidence that was in itself exhilarating to him. He knew, somehow, that he would make good his escape, for the simple reason that there was no room for failure now. A grim smile crept across his lips as a new plan began to take shape in his mind.

Cautiously, he stepped into the corridor and darted onward to a doorway farther along in the direction he had chosen. By this means he finally arrived at another intersection. Before entering it, he heard the running feet of several guards, and he pressed his back to the cold wall, waiting.

Just as the two guards dashed into view, Nad lunged across their path horizontally, and they tripped helplessly on their faces. With a lightning quick movement, Nad leaped into the air and came down with both heels squarely on the head of one of the guards, who went limp in the same instant. The other guard rolled over and lifted his Stun Ray just as Nad kicked him squarely in the face. In the next instant he had acquired their weapons.

With one guard slung over his shoulder, he darted along a new corridor, moving from door to door. Gradually, he neared his objective, which was the disposal room for V sector. As he entered the room, he paused a moment to listen for sounds of pursuit. He could hear the bedlam raised by the sonophones, but nothing else. Then he moved swiftly.

He went to the nearest dumping lock and opened it, dumping his limp burden inside. Then he paused again. His lips tightened as he looked down at the unconscious guard. This was the part of the plan he could little stomach, but it had to be carried out.

Grimly, he braced himself. Then, leaving the lock open, he pulled the disposal valve. There was a roar of escaping air as the guard's body slipped into the vacuum of the disposal chute. The dumping lock door slammed, but did not shut, and air screeched through the remaining crack, making a sound that drowned out the sonophones.

Crawling on his belly against the air blast, Nad got through the doorway of the disposal room before automatic safety devices caused a metal hatch to slide into place, sealing the room hermetically. An alarm gong rang, which he assumed had been installed for such emergencies. He remembered having heard such alarms ring long ago when they said a galactite had pierced the walls. The gong was one of the things he had hoped for. It would bring them to the evidence, which he hoped they would interpret, at least temporarily, as suicide on his part. The other guard he had kicked was dead, so it would take them some time to figure out just who had gone out the disposal tube. He had deliberately left the dump lock door jammed, because a man committing suicide would not have been able to close it from inside. Careful inspection would prove that a human body had gone out the chute, he mused, remembering Gradon's frozen blood on the outer surface of the door of the execution chamber.

"From here," Nad said under his breath, "I've got to disappear."

For hours, however, the Navigators continued their search. Evidently they wanted to find either him or the missing guard, to make the evidence conclusive. As he moved from hiding place to hiding place, he began to lose some of his confidence. The hide and seek could not go on indefinitely. Nor could he fight off a squad of Navigators, once they found him. They might even use the M-Ray on him.

Suddenly, he passed the doorway of a room that was unexpectedly occupied, and someone called out his name. He caught a brief glimpse of an old, gray-haired man with pale blue eyes and a leathery skin, the same who had been present at Gradon's execution. His inclination was to run when he saw the strange weapon the other carried in his hand, but when he realized that the old man was no Navigator he paused and looked back. The old man was in the doorway, beckoning to him.

"Come with me quickly!" he said.

Something told Nad to follow this stranger, and he did. As running feet neared them in the corridor, the old man extinguished the lights of the room and led Nad into the dimness of an inner apartment. There in the wall was a black hole just large enough to squeeze through. The old man went in first and Nad followed. He found himself on a metal catwalk between metal walls. He could feel cables and conduits running in all directions.

The old man closed the opening and fastened several bolts in place. "This is called a maintenance hatch," he explained. "They are very little used nowadays. Most of the Navigators have neglected their knowledge of real maintenance. You'll be safe in here until they really start looking for you."

"Where are we?" said Nad. "And how did you know about this place? Who are you?"

"We are between the walls," came the answer. "This is a vast maze of narrow passages of which the Passengers have no knowledge. I have always known about it because I never lost my memory. I am 'X,' my son, and you have come to me just in time."

CHAPTER THREE

SO it was that a new phase of Nad's existence actually began. The old man told him his name was Yiddir E-5172-P, but as time went on Nad began to suspect that this was an alias disguising a much more important identity than a mere Passenger. The man knew too much. In fact, as far as Nad was concerned, he was an oracle, willingly supplying him with all the knowledge he could absorb.

Yiddir led him, with amazing self-confidence and sure-footedness, through narrow, incomprehensible labyrinths and across dizzying catwalks below which gaped dark recesses the depths of which he could not guess. If what he had known before was a world unto itself, so was this. He seemed to be making a journey born of delirium, into the heart and veins and bowels of a monstrous, living creature.

Everywhere Yiddir had reason to use new words to describe what he saw. There were "control relays" and "power cut-offs" and "master circuits" and "reactor shields," and things incomprehensible without end, until Nad's brain hurt.

Finally, they arrived at Yiddir's destination, his private little citadel. It was an empty chemical tank into which he had diverted a tap from the ventilating system. There were small lockers for supplies of food and water and a few simple articles of furniture. A mattress, a small chair, a box that served as a table, and so on. But there were objects of a more technical nature that went beyond Nad's understanding. He could understand the glow tubes Yiddir had rigged for lighting purposes, and the visiplate and sonophone and even their accompanying converter switches, but one whole end of the tank was a workshop containing a jumble of instruments and equipment that was totally foreign to him. He only grasped that in this secret chamber a very advanced person had lived and worked for perhaps many years of time. Here, at last, was the knowledge and the help he sought. This was the home of "X."

When they had both rested somewhat, Yiddir began to talk to him in earnest, and for Nad the time for great revelations was at hand.

"Have you any concept of what a year of time is?" Yiddir asked him.

"Only that it is a very long period—part of a lifetime, I guess."

"You could not conceive of a period of five hundred years, could you?"

"Perhaps six or seven lifetimes?" Nad suggested.

"Something like that," Yiddir replied. "Well, five hundred years ago, we human beings lived on real worlds; indeed, even three hundred years ago. I'll tell you later what those worlds were like, but suffice it to say, they were natural worlds incalculably larger than this ship you are now in. There were three worlds of principal importance, from which all Passengers and Navigators are descended. There were Venus, Earth and Mars, together with other less developed worlds, revolving each in its own elliptical path about a flaming ball of fire which gave us all the heat and energy necessary to life. This huge ball of fire, men referred to as the sun. Actually, it was one of innumerable similar suns called stars which in turn composed what was called the galaxy.

"Well, to make a long story short, hundreds of millions of people like you and me lived and prospered in a high form of civilization, and we were able to travel between Venus, Earth and Mars at will, for those distances were as nothing when compared with interstellar distances—that is—the distance between the stars.

"It was about five hundred years ago that men first knew that the solar system, of which Venus, Earth and Mars formed a part, was going to be destroyed by cataclysm. That is a runaway star was moving rapidly toward our sun, and it was accurately calculated that within three hundred years the collision would definitely occur.

"This single fact bound our three worlds together with a single purpose in mind—to salvage the human race. To do this, it was considered necessary to invent a way of traversing the awful distance between the stars. Not only would it be necessary to go to the nearer stars but onward indefinitely, if necessary, searching for a life-giving sun in whose system of planets there was at least one world that would be suitable as a new starting place for our kind. It would be necessary to extract cosmic energy from space and convert it into all desirable forms of matter, synthesizing out of basic elements all the molecular compounds necessary to the continuation of life. In short, the ships that were to save humanity had to be worlds independent of all other sources of sustenance except cosmic energy, itself.

"The task seemed insurmountable at first, but the concentrated minds of thousands of our great scientists gradually evolved the required miracle, over the course of the next century and a half. Necessity forced upon Man a superman technology, and the great arks began to be built. As you may have guessed, you are a Passenger in one of them now. It took all the human resources of three worlds to build a hundred of these vessels in as many years. They are flying planets. They move at a speed greater than light, itself. This means that light trying to reach us from behind can never catch up as long as we maintain such a velocity, and light meeting us head on is shoved clear off the visible spectrum.

The result is that behind us is blackness, ahead is blackness, and to either side of us is a halo-like grayness. We can only navigate by means of instruments, some of which employ energies referred to as second order phenomena, which function many times faster than light.

"Before certain events of which I shall inform you caused the fleet to divide, these arks of space travelled in a broad phalanx, each ship one light year distant from the other, which is equivalent to trillions of kilometers. The entire fleet of arks covered a space of one hundred light years, and even by using second order means of communication it sometimes took years thoroughly to relay messages to all ships. This will give you a small idea of the size of this great attempt on the part of human beings to preserve their species.

"So far, we have been under way for slightly more than two hundred years. We are already many generations descended from those who first started out, and we have traveled about six or seven hundred light years in search of a new home."

"But why haven't we found another world?" asked Nad. "And why have the Navigators deprived us of memory, and why are we executed for asking questions that few can resist asking? How did you, alone, escape the M-Ray, and what is this plan you have spoken of concerning liberation and a new way of life?"

Yiddir smiled, patiently. "One question at a time," he said. "First, it was learned within the first fifty years of this great voyage that our sun and the worlds we lived on were very unique, or rather we were especially adapted to live only under the exact conditions set up for us by Nature in our solar system. Many other suns and planetary systems were examined only to be found unsuitable to our needs. Infrequently did we find those other worlds to be inhabited, and only once were we threatened by alien spaceships, but the only weapon we found it necessary to use against them was our far superior velocity. They could not follow us into the great darkness that lies beyond the speed of light.

"Another fifty year period passed, and yet another, and still we had not found what we were looking for. So the situation was when I was a young man, and even later, when I became Chief Navigator on board this ship."

"You!" cried Nad. "You were the Chief Navigator?" His mind reeled under this new shock of surprise.

"Yes," said Yiddir. "My real name is Korlon E-3-N, but therein lies a tale that is the third and final phase of this brief history I am giving you. You see, the present Navigators are outlaws. They mutinied against me."

"But don't the other ships know that by now?" protested Nad. "How long ago did this happen?"

"Thirty years or more."

"Thirty years! And you've remained hidden ever since?"

"Yes. But let me go on with my story…"

"AT times," Yiddir continued, "there were discoveries or circumstances confronting us that led to considerable argument, either among the Navigators or between Navigators and Passengers. About forty years ago, this ship encountered a region of space that appeared to give very promising signs that our goal had been reached. Analysis of the composition of energy patterns, the quality of nuclear radiations and spectrohelioscopic studies showed us that we were in a group of suns that did not seem to be inimical to life. Only one solar system, a rather large one, was found, which contained several large planets, all heavily populated. The problems that arose were the following. First, the civilizations on the planets we discovered were in a state of advancement almost equivalent to our own, and preliminary communications with them indicated that they would not welcome the influx of an alien race. Therefore, to force a landing would have precipitated a war against far superior numbers of people who possessed weapons that were worthy of our respect. Secondly, the sun at the center of this solar system was not any too young and had long since passed into that stage of evolution which scientists refer to as the disintegrant stage. Of course, our kind of life could have flourished yet for thousands of years there, but at the cost of fighting the increasing deleterious effects of hard radiation.

"In spite of this, our whole fleet divided strongly into two factions, one of which was in favor of invasion whatever the cost. The other faction was in favor of continuing our journey in the hope of discovering a more favorable set of circumstances. As I worked my way up to the highest office on board this ship, I adhered to this latter faction, and I trained my son also to hold this perspective of our situation.

"The opposing faction had almost become resigned to their lot when, ten years beyond the controversial solar system, I made a grave mistake. That was thirty years ago."

Yiddir paused, and his pale blue eyes sought Nad's. He saw there an expression of wonderment and awe, as well as the signs of an utterly insatiable thirst for knowledge.

"I was, like many of the higher officers in charge of the expedition, a research scientist, and my specialty was in the second order phenomena. Out of my research evolved a new weapon—the M-Ray. Under any normal circumstances, this would have been a boon to humanity, from a therapeutic point of view. That is, people suffering from mental strain or great sorrow at the loss of a loved one and so forth could be made to forget either temporarily or permanently what was troubling them. But the M-Ray could also be used as a very formidable weapon. It could cause thousands or even millions of people to lose their memories and become as helpless as infants. Moreover, all alien energy shields we had encountered thus far were only of first order nature and therefore would not have been able to stop the M-Ray. In other words, here was a certain weapon against the inhabitable worlds we had contacted some years before.

"My mistake was to keep my weapon a secret, for the time being, for if I had taken it to the authorities on board our flagship they would now be in a position to cope with the terrible danger that threatens them and all the remaining ships that have not yet been taken over by the mutineers."

Nad interrupted. "Do you mean to say that Sargon's brand of Navigators have a foothold on other ships of the fleet?"

Yiddir nodded in bitter assent. "This has been going on for years," he answered.

"But how—"

"Let me continue. My further mistake was to take several other officers into my confidence, even against the advice of my son, who by now was a much more brilliant scientist than I, and who had contributed much to the development of the M-Ray.

"It so happened that one of my confidants was actually an opportunist and a sympathizer with the old opposition, but I did not know this at the time. It was this man who betrayed me and succeeded in producing M-Ray weapons superior to my own—and in effective quantity. The achievement went to his head and he gathered around him the most subversive forces among our number that he could find. He planned eventually to overthrow the government of the whole fleet and prepare for himself and his kind a small empire designed to his own tastes. Furthermore, his plan was to return to the inhabited planets in question and to subject all those races of people to M-Rays in preparation for occupation by his own forces. Even if it came to a matter of subjugating only a part of the fleet and turning back secretly, leaving the other portion to its own destinies, he was determined to carry the plan out.

"Again, my son sought to advise me. He argued that he and I must escape before it was too late. This ship, as you should know, is equipped with life boats which are capable of carrying a hundred or so Passengers. It was my son's plan to steal one of these and travel to the flagship, ten light years distant. Using second order type drive, this journey would have taken several years, but he was certain we could and should make it. Furthermore, he advised me that he was on the trail of just the discovery that would save the fleet government. He was close to developing a second order shield against the M-Ray, and he was confident he could complete it on board a friendly vessel such as the flagship.

"Having learned our lesson in caution by bitter experience, we decided each to take a lifeboat, so that if one of us were apprehended the other might still have a chance of making it.

"Just before we left, however, the Navigators, under their new leader, began their mutiny, and my son and I had to take refuge among the Passengers, whom we enlightened thoroughly concerning the whole situation. It was they who helped us affect our escape, although we were pursued. And we left behind us a ship caught in the throes of a grim war between Navigators and Passengers.

"I succeeded in distracting our pursuers sufficiently, I believe, to help my son escape, but in the process of escaping, myself, my ship was damaged, and after the pursuers abandoned the chase and gave me up for lost, I drifted about almost helplessly. It took me about three months to repair the damage and about a year to find the ship again.

"I was content to return here, because I knew that the Passengers and many of my old friends among the Navigators had by now been subjected to the M-Ray. Despite all rationalization, I felt responsible, not only as inventor of the

M-Ray, but as the captain of my ship—a ship that had mutinied and was the seat of an unlawful government that planned to overthrow the fleet and eventually wage war on innocent worlds, subjugating millions of people to dictatorial rule.

"As one registered as dead, I enjoyed a particular advantage. Also, I had not lost my memory, and I knew the ship better than any Navigator on board. For years I have lived in secrecy, but a relatively short time ago something new developed that made it necessary for me to disguise myself as a Passenger. It was an easy matter for me to forge identifications and even place corroborative records in the files of the Navigators. Thus I created Yiddir E-5172-P, an inconsequential Passenger who was free to move about among you and select his allies. For my present venture I need about one hundred men and women, and I have long since chosen you as my principal aide."

"Me? Why pick on me?"

Yiddir smiled. "Look back on your actions that led to your escape today. Need you ask me more questions? I was not quite prepared to affect your escape according to my own well laid plans, and yet when your emergency arose you were capable of taking care of yourself."

Nad disregarded the compliment. "But did your son ever reach the flagship?" he asked.

Yiddir shrugged, resignedly. "How can I tell? I can intercept communications from the other arks, but I dare not try to transmit, for fear of discovery. All I have learned is that a new Fleet Governor is in charge of the flagship, who is apparently unaware of what has been going on here. However, he seems to be a very capable man. His name is Nor E-I-M. I should certainly like to contact him sometime, for I am sure he would make a worthy ally. But that would take years, and there is no time for that just now."

"But what about the mutineers' plan to turn back to the solar system they wanted to invade? When will they do that?"

Yiddir waved his hand. "My story is not yet at an end," he said, patiently. "Listen to me carefully…"

CHAPTER FOUR

"I HAVE not been able to verify all the facts as yet," he continued, "but in rough analysis, the circumstances at present are as follows. The rebel Navigators have taken over a large portion of the fleet, just how much I cannot say, except that I know the flagship is still free and unaware of what has happened. Or else it may be that the rebels fear the flagship of Nor E-I-M, that perhaps some sort of resistance has been demonstrated. Anyway, the fact remains that this rebel portion of the fleet has already broken off from the main fleet, come to a stop, and turned back toward the solar system they plan to invade. It will take years to retrace those many light years of distance, but they are determined to do it. Meanwhile, the portion of the fleet that is still under Fleet Government is drawing further away from us all the time in the original direction taken by the expedition. Now, between our group of rebel arks and the Fleet Government arks lies the goal I am after. Listen...

"At the time that we slowed up to turn back, of course light from the stars was again perceptible and some important observations were made. I know that at that time the astrophysicists on board this particular ship discovered, in our own region of space, an inhabitable world. Oh it was a small one and not overly promising, because it was very young, geographically speaking. It was as yet uninhabited by the most primitive form of man, but was capable of supporting our kind. So mediocre was the find, however, that the rebel government in charge here decided not even to advise the rest of their representatives on board the other conquered ships. And of course the Fleet Government ships remained unadvised and were allowed to proceed on their way.

"However, it was the result of my own analysis of that region of space that stirred me into action. My own instruments revealed to me that there are other systems nearby that should have been investigated. I know this ship did some searching, but the job was not thorough, and they gave it up in order to keep pace with the other rebel ships now en route to the inhabited solar systems they intended to invade.

"Now, therefore, my immediate plan of action is this. In the lifeboat lockers are, as I have mentioned before, many ships, each of which is capable of transporting a hundred Passengers with reasonable comfort. As they are capable of converting cosmic energy into matter and synthesizing just like the ark does, they can support human life as indefinitely as their mother ship. It is my plan to use one of those ships and affect the escape of about a hundred Passengers, preferably young men and women, and make our way back to that small, primitive world that the Navigators discovered, and establish a base there for further exploration to discover the other solar system or systems that my instruments have indicated must exist in that region. If we fail, at least we will have one small, primitive world at our disposal on which to start a new life. And then if the rebel fleet should meet with surprise opposition and get wiped out, or if the other arks fail in their search, at least our small group will serve to rescue our species from extinction."

Suddenly, Yiddir fell silent, and Nad knew that he had finished. Yet there were still more questions to be asked.

"All this is a fine plan," he said, "and you can never appreciate what it means to me to know at last what this life of ours is all about. What I don't like about your idea, however, is leaving the field wide open for the rebel Navigators such as Sargon and his kind."

"There is one faint possibility," said Yiddir, "that this great new master of the flagship, Nor E-I-M, might be in a position to cope with the rebels, but there is the risk that if I were to beam a communication to him, once we have made good our escape, it might be intercepted and result in precipitating on the Fleet Government a battle for which they are not prepared. I feel that it would be better not to take that risk, to let each segment of the fleet go its own way, so that there will be two chances of survival instead of one. Nor E-I-M has been hailed as a scientific genius, and I know that his section of the fleet is in good hands."

"It is too bad that your son, with his secret of M-Ray defense, could not have joined forces with Nor," said Nad. "It is obvious he did not, because if he had done so, by now the Fleet Government would have taken action against the rebels."

Yiddir sighed. "That too, is my conviction," he said. "I have lost my son."

Nad reached out and squeezed Yiddir's frail hand. "May I serve R3 a poor substitute?" he asked.

Yiddir's old face brightened. He grasped Nad's hand with both of his. "Substitute, no," he said. "You *are* my son, from this day forward."

"Thanks," Nad replied. "But there's just one thing you're not going to like."

"What is that?"

"I am not a complete altruist like you. I harbor a bitter hatred that must be satisfied. Before I leave here, I intend to throttle one Sargon M-13-NT."

Yiddir shook his head in disapproval. "You must forget that," he admonished. "Sargon is in high favor among the rebels. To expose yourself to him again would be to endanger the whole plan. You must learn to subordinate personal desires to the importance of your mission. Don't you think that I, too, was long tempted by vengeful desire? *This is my ship!*" Yiddir's eyes flashed anger. "But I held onto myself, and I pride myself that I acted in the best interests of the majority. I expect you to do the same."

The muscles lumped along Nad's jaws, and he clenched his fists, but he controlled himself. "All right," he grumbled. "Let's get to work on this plan of yours."

Yiddir beamed with pride and satisfaction. "That's the spirit, son. Self-control is your most strategic weapon now."

WHEN Nad and Yiddir acted, they worked swiftly. Contact was made with certain other Passengers on Yiddir's long prepared list, chiefly by means of individually activated sonophones. In the privacy of his own room, a likely recruit was addressed as follows:

"The day of liberation has arrived. You have been chosen to join us. We are returning to a natural world and a natural way of life. We have both the knowledge and the means. What was taken from your minds, your rightful heritage, will be restored by a complete revelation of the truth of your origin and your purpose. There is no time for questions. We must act swiftly. Go and contact ten of your friends, five of them young men and five of them young women. Caution them all to strictest secrecy or this whole plan will fail and your last chance will have been sacrificed. These ten people will contact only you. You have three hours to accomplish this. So act at once! When you are ready, or at the end of three hours maximum, bring your people to your own reception room and there you will be guided into liberation."

In the course of an hour, Nad and Yiddir thus contacted eight key men and women. It was almost time for them to start leading the first contacts and their recruits through various maintenance hatches between the walls when Nad finally tried to contact Lylwani.

Yldra was with Ron, in Ron's reception room. This time, Nad dared to activate the visiplate as well as the sonophone.

"Nad!" cried Yldra, leaping to her feet. "Where are you? We thought you were either captured or dead!"

"There is no time to explain," he said, while his eyes searched the room through the two-way visiplate. "Where is Lylwani?"

"We don't know," said Yldra. "After you escaped from the guards she disappeared."

Then Ron found his voice. "I think she tried some crazy scheme to save you, and the Navigator's probably have her by now. Maybe Sargon."

"*Sargon!*" Nad's face blanched and his mouth tightened. "It can't be—not now, not at a time like this. She's got to be here. There's no time to lose!"

Quickly, he gave them his recruiting message, with extra explanations to help reassure Ron, and he deputized Yldra to gather up some of her friends.

The effect on Yldra was astonishing to Nad. As he told her the news, she seemed to come alive as though all her previous life had been lived in a shadow world. Now she seemed to perceive reality for the first time. In spite of her naturally pale Venusian complexion, a new color leaped to her cheeks and he eyes flashed with little fires of wild, new energy.

She turned to Ron and flung her arms around his neck. "Ron!" she cried. "It's come true at last! There is another world and another life. Nad's dream has come true. Quick! Let's go get Nilra and Gorn and Myrla and—"

She stopped, amazed, because Ron did not reflect any of her mood. Sweat stood out on his forehead and his mouth was agape, his eyes round with fear…

"They'll kill us all!" he cried out. "It's mutiny! I'm innocent!" he yelled. "Innocent, do you hear. I want none of it. I want to stay right here!"

"*Ron!*" shouted Nad, in a tone which he seldom used with his brother. "Shut your mouth and don't speak another word. If you are so afraid of death, then remember this. Open your mouth once more as you have done just now and I will kill you myself..."

Ron was left speechless, as was Yldra.

"I can't help it, Yldra," Nad explained. "There is too much at stake. The whole future of humanity may be ruined by that sniveling coward. You keep him quiet if you want him to live or join us at all. Now hurry and assemble your friends in this room as quickly as you can. I'll give you two hours. In the meantime, I'm going to find Lylwani..."

KRYLORNO, the poet, was a vain and sensitive man. Secretly, he resented the fact that no woman had as yet gone with him to the authorities to request permission for cohabitation. He was older than the crowd he chose to associate with by some ten years, but he did everything possible to conceal the difference as it was one of the sore points of his vanity. Another blow to his vanity was Yldra's inexplicable attachment to Ron. To think that she should prefer that club-footed, worthless coward to him!

He was thinking of these things when Ron and Yldra approached him. It was on one of the refreshment mezzanines overlooking the great Recreation Hall. Many of his previous "suicide" group were there, but they had become divorced from their fanaticism by the unprecedented message of "X." Since that moment a great, secret unrest had manifested itself among the Passengers. The Navigators had been able to gather that certain of the Passengers were discussing some great secret that they were somewhat unwilling to share with others of their number, and general Passenger speculation was running wild. The Navigators, suspecting that the whole thing was merely another manifestation of general discontent, had resorted to an experiment. They had released a previous ban on alcoholic refreshments, and the effect, in general, had been favorable already.

Whereas most of the Passengers had become cheerful, Krylorno had become more moody and sensitive than usual, and was consuming liquor in large amounts. Yldra's entrance with Ron was, therefore, the spark that kindled the smoldering fire.

When Yldra tried to engage certain younger members of the party in private conversation, he resented it at once. Also, his curiosity was piqued by the transformation that had come over her. Her face was radiant; her eyes flashed new life and vigor, as though her existence had taken on new meaning. She spoke rapidly and excitedly, but it was obvious that he, Krylorno, was being excluded deliberately.

Somewhat erratically, he walked over to her table with his half-filled glass. Everyone stopped talking as he began to give her a toast:

"She's made of dreams, or so it seems.

"For when she speaks to me.

"My thoughts are stilled and my heart is thrilled.

"With a dreamy ecstasy;

"And in her eyes my reason dies.

"And I am prison bound—"

He paused, with upraised glass, scowling at her and the others.

"I swear," he said. "If you don't all look as though you resented my presence..."

No one said a word. Some hung their heads or looked away.

"Why!" he said, not pleadingly, but challengingly. "What is this secret business all about? Has the voice of 'X' been haunting you again from out of the Abyss? Has he said you shall exclude Krylorno from the great liberation?"

Yldra paled because Krylorno was shouting these words recklessly. She got to her feet quickly and came close to him. Her small hand clamped down over his mouth.

"Krylorno, listen to me," she said, softly. "You spoke to me recently, great words about courage. You have demonstrated to everyone that you care for me. Now I am asking you to prove both. For my sake, and for the sake of all our kind, be still! This is the time of salvation for a few. There is neither time nor room for more. Perhaps your time will come later, but for the present Nad says they should all be young—"

"Young!" Krylorno fired back, "What do you think I am—an octogenarian?"

Again the small hand closed his lips and her dark eyes sought his, pleadingly. Finally, he shrugged.

"All right, children," he said, patronizingly. "What difference does it make, after all? A lifetime of certain boredom or a brief struggle for a dream that must end in certain death for all of you. Condemn me to boredom if you will." He smiled mockingly at them. "I congratulate you!" he said, lifting his glass. "It is not every day that one may die for a heroic cause…"

Ron broke, at last. He threw himself on Krylorno, terrified.

"Take my place!" he exclaimed. "Go with Yldra. She's going to take the others to my unit, where Nad will contact them. Take my place!" he cried. "I don't want to go. I'm innocent! I want no part of it!"

Krylorno cocked an eyebrow at him in theatrical disdain, and Yldra scowled for the first time since anyone could remember.

"Ron," she said, icily, "you had better hope Nad did not hear you over the sonophone. He *would* kill you. Remember his warning. It is evident your words to me of love and devotion were false, or you would want to be with me."

Ron broke down completely. He sat at a table and buried his head in his arms.

"I do love you, Yldra," he sobbed, "but I'm a coward. I can't help being what I am."

Yldra made a sign to several of the young men beside her, and they moved to obey. They picked Ron up bodily and carried him. He screamed, once, and they knocked him senseless.

Left alone, Krylorno bathed his internal wounds with alcohol. The drunker he became, the more distorted was his reasoning, until he was filled with bitter resentment.

"Leave me out, will they?" he said, staggering to his feet. "Ha! I'll teach them not to slight Krylorno!"

Bottle in hand, he staggered in the general direction of section N, to find a Navigator.

BY this time, Yiddir was busy leading various groups of recruits through maintenance hatches and guiding them to a safe rendezvous between the walls. He became very apprehensive as Nad's quota failed to appear, however. Suspecting that something was wrong, he deputized certain young men to guard the others and keep them quiet, and then he moved swiftly to take in Nad's groups.

When at last he came to Yldra's group, he questioned them, through the visiplate, concerning Nad. When he learned that the latter had gone searching for Lylwani in section N, a shadow of grave disappointment fell across his aged countenance.

"We cannot wait," he said. "All of you enter the first apartment of this unit, quickly."

"But this is a bachelor's unit," protested one of the girls.

"Forget all the laws the Navigators ever taught you, if you value your life," said Yiddir. "Go quickly!"

Yiddir led the last of the recruits through a maintenance hatch. Just as he was fastening it behind him, however, the whole ark began to resound with alarm bells.

"What is that?" Yldra asked him, close by his shoulder.

Yiddir's old hands trembled as he tightened the last bolt. "Perhaps our plan has been discovered," he said. "Listen!"

The sonophones were raising a bedlam. *"All guard units report immediately to T.H.Q."* came the announcement.

"T.H.Q. means Technical Headquarters," said Yiddir. "And only Technical knows anything about this area of the ship we are in. I think they are after us. We must move immediately to the life boat lockers. Follow me!"

"But Nad—and Lylwani!" protested Yldra.

"Casualties," said Yiddir, coldly. "Forget them or you'll all be caught. There is too much at stake now. Come on, quickly, all of you!"

CHAPTER FIVE

NAD DID not try to excuse himself for disobeying Yiddir's admonition to subordinate personal desires to the welfare of the majority. When it came to leaving Lylwani in Sargon's clutches—forever, never to see her again—his rationalizations ceased and instinct took over. In a blind, reckless rage, he sought Sargon out.

By following the catwalks forward, he soon reached section N, and at his first opportunity he began unfastening one of the now familiar safety hatches. Yiddir had armed him with both an M-Ray and a Disruptor. In the mood he was in, he was prepared to M-Ray all Navigators into a state of complete idiocy; or blast the whole section to atoms, if necessary.

When he came through the hatch he fixed it so that it was unfastened while appearing not to have been disturbed. This would be his exit, he hoped.

He found himself in a vault-like room that was a maze of instruments, some whirring and ticking, others flickering with kaleidoscope colors. Quickly, he tried *the door* of the chamber and found it could only be opened from the outside. So he blasted it with the Disruptor.

Once outside, he found himself in a shining corridor, face to face with a young Navigator who was paralyzed with shock. Evidently, nothing of this nature had ever occurred in his lifetime. To see an armed Passenger come blasting his way out of the recording vault was too much for him.

By the time he had recovered, he found himself covered with a hot-barreled Disruptor, and he was looking into a pair of cold gray eyes that said simply: *Obey or die!*

"Take me to Sargon," said Nad. "No questions. Quick!" He jabbed the Navigator and the latter moved without saying a word.

Two more Navigators turned into the corridor ahead of them. They were armed guards, Sargon's own men. In spite of their surprise, they raised their Stun Rays almost simultaneously.

But Nad's M-Ray was on them, and their weapons lowered suddenly to dangle ludicrously from their fingertips. They grinned idiotically as Nad and the now fully terrified Navigator passed them. Nad acquired one of the Navigators' Stun Rays and thrust it into his belt.

"I'm your man," the Navigator with him whispered. "Just don't M-Ray me. I swear I won't double cross you…"

"Shut up and keep moving—fast," Nad hissed. "How much farther is it?"

"Here…" The Navigator pointed to a large metal door on Nad's right.

Whereupon Nad extracted the Stun Ray from his belt. "This won't hurt," he whispered. The other slumped quietly to the floor, blissfully unconscious.

Nad tried Sargon's door and found it to be unlocked. Then he flung it open and sprang into the middle of the room.

The first thing he focused his eyes on was Lylwani, herself, sitting up in her cushioned chair as though paralyzed with amazement. Obviously she had been crying, for her usually clear green eyes were bloodshot and their lids were swollen.

Now her eyes widened and an incredulous cry rose to her lips, but Nad instantly signaled her to be quiet. He turned and dragged into the room the inert body of the Navigator he had stunned, and he closed the door behind him. Then he beckoned Lylwani to him.

She sprang to her feet and came into his arms, trembling on the edge of hysteria. "My darling," she whispered. "You're safe…you're safe…"

"Far from it," he said. "We've got to get out of here. Where's Sargon?"

"I don't know. He told me you had killed yourself, so I gave up all hope of ever—"

"Never mind, honey. Let's go."

Then he stopped in his tracks as alarm bells started ringing everywhere. The sonophone in the room boomed a torrent of excited orders.

"Come on!" he said, opening the door to the corridor. But when he looked out he knew his way was blocked. The corridor was filled with running guards.

"Oh Nad!" cried Lylwani. "What can we do now?"

"Plenty," he said, locking the door from inside. "Follow me…"

He took her by the hand and led her into an inner compartment that composed Sargon's private quarters. Unfortunately he did not find the usual maintenance hatch.

The two looked at each other. The din raised by the alarms; the bellowing of the sonophones and the sound of many running feet began to increase the beating of their pulses, and terror found a grip on their hearts.

Just then, guards outside in the corridor began to pound on Sargon's office door.

Lylwani clutched at Nad's arms and pressed her head tightly against his chest. "You tried, darling," she said. "It's all right. We'll go out together."

"That's right," he said, grimly, "We'll go out together. Get behind me…"

When she stepped wonderingly behind him, he focused his Disruptor on the wall of the apartment. There was a white flash accompanied by an explosion, and Lylwani saw a ragged hole leading into unknown darkness.

"What is it?" she whispered in awe. "The Abyss?"

"No. It is the road to the Abyss—and freedom. Follow me!"

Soon it became apparent that Navigators had entered between the walls, because he could hear them shouting, and their voices echoed and reechoed eerily through the dark and narrow labyrinths. Far ahead of him, Nad heard a series of startled shouts and screams.

"They've found them," he muttered. "They're fighting—probably being M-Rayed. Come on, quickly, or we're lost forever!"

At that precise moment, a booted foot kicked Nad's light out of his hand and darkness engulfed him. At the same time, he felt his M-Ray being snatched out of his grip.

Viciously, he sprayed the whole area in front of him and to each side with Stun Ray, and silence filled in the darkness to completion. Aside from dim and distant sounds of fighting, he could only hear Lylwani's frightened breathing and his own. He felt the walls on either side of him and found them to be of a strange, warm substance that he had felt once before when Yiddir first guided him between the walls.

Suddenly, from above his head, a voice said, "I have this M-Ray focused on both of you. Don't move!"

As the two looked up into the apathetic glare of Nad's own flashlight, they did not have to see who was there above it in the darkness. The voice was that of Sargon.

Nad swiftly analyzed his predicament. He and Lylwani stood on a narrow catwalk between the walls. Below them was a black pit of emptiness. Above, somewhere deadly close, crouched Sargon. And far away somewhere Yiddir and the recruits struggled with the Navigators.

Whatever was to be done had to be done instantly or the whole cause was lost. But Sargon had an M-Ray focused on him, and there came to Nad's mind all too clearly the full evaluation of his danger in regard to that weapon.

If Sargon activated it, Nad and perhaps Lylwani also would lose all memory of life, their purpose, their hopes and plans, their love for each other, their conditionings, their personalities—their very identity. A wave of real terror engulfed him, but he fought it, strengthened at last by one element in his blood and marrow that was unfailing—his hatred, of Sargon.

"In my hand," he said quietly to Sargon, "I hold a Disruptor. I believe you know better than I do whether or not there is an instant of awareness before the mind succumbs to the M-Ray. In that instant, if you use it on me, I will blast you into extinction, as well as a good portion of the ship."

There was a tantalizing silence, except that Nad heard Sargon breathing tensely above him. He also felt Lylwani's tightened grip on his arm.

"Lylwani," he said, divining Sargon's thoughts, "if you feel the M-Ray, grip my arm as hard as you can."

Sargon said, "You also have some reason for not using your weapons."

"Yes," Nad replied, every sense tingling with alertness. "The Stun Ray might miss." He realized that the action of using the Stun Ray might allow the brief instant of awareness of the M-Ray to come and pass, leaving him helpless. "Furthermore," he said, "we are standing between two reactor shields." Yiddir had tried to explain what lay behind these weird shields, but all Nad had understood was that something of monstrous power lay harnessed there. "You can appreciate better than I," he said to Sargon, "what would happen if the Disruptor were to penetrate these shields."

"It would blow this whole ark to blazes," said Sargon coldly.

"Then don't force me to use it in this spot," countered Nad. "Drop that M-Ray and get out of here!"

There was another moment of intense silence, while Nad nervously fingered his Stun Ray and Lylwani still gripped him with a feverish tenacity. Sweat trickled around the trigger finger of Nad's other hand, where it rested on the Disrupter release. The roaring of his pulse drowned out the more distant sounds of alarm and fighting. He marveled, in spite of his predicament, at the degree of tenseness to which the mind could be brought without breaking down.

Finally, slowly and calmly, Sargon spoke. "It's Lylwani I want," he said. "I'll take every risk you will, so listen to this, if you want to help your friends down there, leave Lylwani here and go. If you don't like that proposition—"

There was no more room for words.

Nad fired the Stun Ray upward as rapidly as his hand could work, but in the same moment he yelled as Lylwani's fingernails tore his flesh. Simultaneously, Sargon's heavy body thumped unconscious onto the cat-walk.

Nad placed his weapons in his belt and reached down with hungry hands to find the other's throat. But he was too late to prevent the body from slipping off the catwalk into nothingness.

"Lylwani!" he called. Groping behind him, he found her and clutched her to him, kissing her face and lips. "You're safe! We'll make it yet!"

Then his flesh crept and he felt his hair bristling. For Lylwani only giggled at him and made nameless sounds in reply...

NAD could never quite remember how he found his way to the lifeboat lockers, even though Yiddir had already shown him the way.

Vaguely, he recalled interminable periods of balancing precariously on dark catwalks with Lylwani in his arms, or of hiding while Navigators led the poor recruits back into captivity, passing him close by, with lights, so that he could see the victims' idiotic smiles. They had all been M-Rayed like his beloved Lylwani. The whole plan was at an end, he had thought dimly.

Except for himself and Lylwani.

He had an irrational desire to risk it in one of the space boats alone with her, somehow to master the secret of the controls and in spite of having no knowledge of astronomy whatsoever to find that little lost world of which Yiddir had told him. There he would reeducate his sweetheart and they would live and reproduce their own kind.

With these dim, mad thoughts and with Lylwani lying childlike in his arms, he arrived at the lockers. There he saw lights and Navigator guards, a squad of ten of them who had made one fatal mistake, Nad perceived. They were all gathered together in one small group.

Suddenly, his reason became twisted between insupportable grief and a reckless thirst for revenge. He set Lylwani down and deliberately aimed his Disruptor at the guards, firing without warning.

There followed a quick succession of blinding flashes and deafening explosions. Not only the guards went into nothingness, but several spaceboats, as well, along with part of the metal floor. Fortunately, the great cryosite doors separating the lockers from the Abyss held, although the inner sections of the two airlocks were destroyed.

He stood there, wondering if he was going to vomit. Behind him, Lylwani laughed and clapped her hands gaily at the fireworks and the smoldering results. Nad did not look back at her. He stood alone in the broken desolation of the place, trying to swallow a lump in his throat that threatened to choke him.

Then, suddenly, he felt a friendly hand on his arm and a voice said. "Follow us quickly." It was Yiddir.

Nad's mind was reeling from the impact of events too terrible and swift to assimilate. He heard Yldra's voice crying out in the darkness behind him as she discovered Lylwani's plight, and there were a few other male voices, but he cared not whether they were of friend or foe, of sane man or idiot. He followed blindly.

THERE were other space boats and launching locks that were still intact, although one thing bothered Yiddir that he refrained from mentioning to the others. He observed a very curious thing about one of the launching locks, but paused there for only a brief moment. Then, grimly, he led his pitifully small party onward. There was no time for conversation. The Navigators would be back in a matter of moments.

The dark ship lay enigmatically in its lock—a question mark standing between precarious Today and a totally unknown *Tomorrow*. Failure, privation, recapture, endless wandering through blackness and into madness? Sudden, violent, merciful death? All these questions were equally unanswerable as they filed silently on board and Yiddir turned to the control room.

No one was curious about the interior of this ark of freedom for which they had fought and for which scores of their companions had sacrificed their personalities. To them it was shelter. They tied themselves into cushioned seats as Yiddir instructed them to do—and they waited.

Yiddir had not wasted his thirty years of hidden exile. He had studied all controls and every phase of maintenance with painstaking care, and now he knew more about these space boats than the best Navigator on board the mother vessel. Expertly, he activated the lock and caused the outer doors to slide open, exposing the lifeboat to the awful gulf of blackness outside. For one brief moment his hand paused on the control. For centuries, his kind had been bottled up in darkness, except for sporadic half-forgotten intervals. He felt suddenly the weight of Man's loneliness, lost as they all were in the far reaches of the unknown galaxy. He knew that this single lifeboat, once detached from its base, would be like an electron lost in the farthest depths of the Seventh Sea.

With an unaccustomed prayer on his lips, he launched the boat outward into the great darkness...

CHAPTER SIX

THEIR little group consisted of seven. Ron, Yldra, Lylwani, Gorn and Karg. Gorn was a pale, blue-haired Venusian like Yldra. Karg was one of Lylwani's race—a Martian. Gorn had been wounded by a bad fall from one of the catwalks. Two ribs had punctured his left lung and he was dying from a pulmonary hemorrhage.

He was bitterly contemptuous of Ron. Just before he died, on that first day out, he called everybody around him and addressed Ron in their presence. In his dimming eyes they could see most of those qualities that they needed so desperately for their venture—courage, strength, and a full awareness of the role they were all acting in the destiny of their kind.

"Ron," he said, laboriously, "I want you to witness my death and realize what it means. This expedition could well be the only chance for survival of the human race. Of course, you may all die and one or both branches of the fleet may succeed. But it's just as possible that the reverse may happen. Here there is no room for a coward!" His emphasis on this last phrase cost him a new pain and he almost fainted. "I want you to realize that your outburst to Krylorno was directly responsible for the failure of the others to reach this ship. Thanks to you, about eighty-five recruits, young men and women, have been deprived of their memories just like Lylwani here. If this thought haunts you through the days or years ahead as you seek a new world. I hope it serves to cure you of your cowardice. My death is also your fault, Ron. So you are responsible for taking my place in this party." His eyes closed and his whole body tensed. "Take over—Ron!"

These were his last words.

As Yiddir decelerated as much as he could within the limits of reasonable comfort, the invisible mother ship and the rest of the rebel fleet receded at the rate of millions of kilometers each minute; in an opposite direction the distant Government Fleet still flung its light years long phalanx into ever expanding vastness; and he and his handful of lost souls were totally detached from all things kindred. They were like the first seeds of life in the Beginning, or like the last dust of the ages settling in the sunset of Creation. Whether colossal Nature would be mother or nemesis to them was a question that would remain unanswered through long months or even years to come. Yiddir was without hope, because of their small number, but where hope ran out, life continued. Almost like a robot, he went forward with the plan. He decelerated, day after day and week after week, calculating that their velocity would be reduced to that of the speed of light within two months. Then, for the first time in years, he would see the stars. It would be the first glimpse for the rest on board, and he wondered if that over-whelming spectacle would inspire them, or depress them with a sense of utter futility.

Then, too, there was that strange mystery concerning the lifeboat locker. After he had brooded on it for days, he finally called Nad to his side.

"What happened to Sargon?" he asked him, without preamble. "You said you overcame him in a struggle, during which he M-Rayed Lylwani. But what are the details? How did you overcome him?"

Mention of Sargon never failed to key Nad's faculties to a maximum of alertness. He quickly perceived that Yiddir was driving at something.

"Why?" he asked, his gray eyes meeting Yiddir's steadily. "I got him with a Stun Ray and he fell off the catwalk."

Yiddir stared back intently. "How far did he fall?"

"I don't know. It was dark. Why do you ask?"

"The effects of the Stun Ray only last a few minutes, depending on the intensity for which the weapon is set. It may be—"

He paused, thinking. Then he asked, "Did Sargon really care a great deal about Lylwani?"

"He told me he would take every risk I would to get her."

"Hmmm... That might be the motive. He certainly wouldn't take such a risk in the line of mere duty, or even for revenge alone. But if Lylwani means as much to him as she does to you... Tell me this. Did he know she was M-Rayed?"

"No. But what are you driving at?"

Yiddir spoke very slowly. "The spaceboat locker next to ours was empty," he said, "yet only six hours before our departure I know there was a ship sitting in it. That can only mean that very shortly before we left another ship also came out. It may be out here somewhere right now, trailing us."

Nad's excitement subsided slightly. "Sargon could have recovered in time to get to the lockers ahead of us," he said. "And he could have gone out into the Abyss to trap us in case we escaped. But in that case he would have spotted us immediately on his instruments and struck long before this. His stake in the rebellion is too important to be abandoned, I think, even for Lylwani."

"That is an admirable deduction," said Yiddir. "But perhaps he might know how to take Lylwani and return to the rebel fleet as well."

"What! Return to the fleet from here? There *is* no return!"

"Yes," said Yiddir. "I have never told you, and you must never tell the others, but there is a way. Our drivers can be altered for more speed. It is possible to overtake the fleet, although as the distance increases the time factor increases proportionately. Sargon is a capable Navigator and I know he finished Technical in order to increase his rating. He would know how to convert the drivers. Higher velocities haven't been resorted to, in general, because the occasional meteors getting through our detection screens would have dangerous mass, enough to penetrate cryosite walls.

"But—why should Sargon wait this long to strike?"

"I don't know. Maybe a new factor has been added that delayed him. A breakdown, or some accident."

"But all that is pure supposition. Haven't you some sort of detector on board? Can't you tell if he is out here?"

"Within ten million kilometers or so, yes. Much, much time has elapsed, and distances are tremendous out here. He could be on our trail without our knowing it."

"But if we couldn't detect him, how could he detect us in this darkness?"

"The answer to that is simpler than you think," said Yiddir. "You forget that he knows where we are going."

Nad's brows raised and his mouth parted. "How could he?" he asked. "I'll admit he'd know all about the world we're trying to reach, but why should he assume we know about it?"

Yiddir shrugged. "I don't know how much Yldra said in front of Krylorno or how much Krylorno told the Navigators. But one thing is certain. No Passenger could handle this ship as I have. It takes technical training which, incidentally, I am going to have to give to you and Ron and Karg as soon as possible. The Navigators have always specu-lated on my escape and that of my son, years ago. They have always feared that perhaps one of us would return, either alone or in force. Krylorno's tale would easily enable them to guess what happened. They knew at once that I was on board. Well, that may be one thing that has made Sargon cautious, if he has followed us. He knows, perhaps, that he not only has another full-fledged Navigator to deal with, but the former captain of the ark—and a man of legendary scientific ability, in fact, the inventor of the M-Ray. The more I think of it, the more it all seems to fit together. That missing lifeboat in the locker next to ours cannot be disregarded."

Nad sat silently for a long time, gazing with narrowed eyes into space. "What could he do if he decided to take us?" he asked, finally.

"Our meteor detectors would give us warning. We have shields against all primary rays and the Disrupter cannons, which the rebels have mounted in all these boats. I doubt if he knows enough about second order stuff to assemble an effective M-Ray projector, which he would have to have, because the hand M-Ray is only good at short range. I have no shield against a good M-Ray projector. Only my son knew that secret, and he is long since gone."

"Then what can Sargon do?"

"I don't know. That may be why he's holding back— perhaps trying to figure something out. Perhaps—"

"What?"

"Perhaps he would even go so far as to follow us to that little planet of ours and kidnap Lylwani when the opportunity presented itself."

Nad got to his feet. "I think we're both dreaming," he said. "Why don't you start teaching me what you know about this ship?"

Yiddir sat still, thinking for a long time. Then he looked up and asked, "What do you want first, instruction in piloting—or in the use of the armaments?"

As he looked steadily at Nad, the latter broke into a grim smile. "Okay," Nad said. "Then we're not dreaming. Let me see those Disruptor cannons…"

DECELERATION continued, unabated, and the passengers of the small ship walked in it with heavy and laborious tread. The darkness prevailed, day after day, and each sought to occupy himself to the best of his abilities. Yiddir carefully instructed Nad, Karg and Ron concerning all the controls on board. He even started on a long-range conversion job, working on one of their four drivers at a time. He hoped to utilize the increased velocity someday in their further search for the better solar system whose existence he suspected.

Yldra had been assigned the long, arduous task of reeducating Lylwani. She had to teach her to speak and even how to eat and walk properly. It was a heartbreaking task, but Nad was always there, encouraging her in the depths of each new discouragement.

Karg was indirectly helpful. The short-statured little Martian was naturally cheerful in spite of the discomfiture of doubled gravity due to deceleration. He was interested in everything, quick to learn, and entertaining. But most valuable of all, from the psychological standpoint, he had brought along one precious belonging that was now a means of mental salvation. It was a Martian *querla,* a small musical instrument that generated invisible rays in which his moving fingers produced a marvelous music of rich tone and endless variety. Yldra had a very pleasing voice, and sometimes the two would entertain the others by playing and singing.

At such times Lylwani was very receptive and cooperative, and she even repeated some of Yldra's songs, to Nad's infinite delight. All these things served to establish a routine and way of life for the ship's small company, which provided a certain measure of stability.

But one day—tragedy struck...

CHAPTER SEVEN

ON the upper deck, astern, was an observation chamber equipped with a huge, double-paned window of transparent metal. While they were in the darkness, there was nothing to be seen from this vantage point, but Yiddir had announced that their velocity was being reduced very closely to the speed of light, and that any time now they might begin to see some evidence of the bright universe that had surrounded them invisibly all of their lives.

Ron had been sitting with Yldra in this room, both of them watching the window for some break in the darkness that lay astern. They had spoken of many things, their old acquaintances left behind, and of the possibilities of their future life on the new world.

Suddenly, the sonophone in their chamber brought Nad's voice to them. He reminded Yldra that it was her watch with Lylwani, and she got up to leave.

"I'll stay here a while," Ron told her.

The chamber just forward of the aft observation bridge had been converted into a battle station by the rebel Navigators. Here were mounted several Disruptor cannons. Just as Yldra stepped into this room on her way forward, the galactite struck.

Started on its journey eons past, the small metallic fragment had gathered much more velocity than a meteor. Meteors were local phenomena, occurring within the galaxy, but the galactite was much rarer owing to its extra-galactic origin. In the course of time required for its transit between galaxies, it had acquired a velocity greater than light itself.

The arks of the fleet and the lifeboats could detect the approach of ordinary meteors and automatically vary their courses slightly to avoid them in time, or if a meteor penetrated the detection area and struck, the cryosite hulls could withstand the blow. But no detectors or metal walls could stop a galactite because of its terrible velocity.

The galactite struck the ship and penetrated it like a hot knife passing through butter. In its path it left a series of small, neat, round holes on both sides of the hull and through two decks of cryosite. Its passage was accompanied by a deafening report, which stunned Yldra momentarily.

Then air began to rush out of the chamber she was in. She began to struggle with the forward hatch, but it was jammed as the result of the galactite's titanic blow. She turned aft, but too late, because the observation hatch slid automatically into place, as it had been designed to operate just that way in such an emergency.

Its seal could be released, however, from Ron's side, and she called to him frantically to help her. When half the air had been released from the room, an unexpected phenomenon occurred that gave promise of saving her, even as she slipped into unconscious. The moisture in the air, as it encountered the deep cold of outer space, froze instantly, and soon the galactite holes in the hull were obstructed with ice, which slowed the escape of air. There was still a chance.

Over the sonophone, Yiddir's tense instructions penetrated Ron's panic. "The air in Yldra's chamber is leaking out very slowly," he said. "Open your hatch and pull Yldra through. Then close it again. This will reduce your own air pressure considerably and you may pass out, but you'll be safe. We are putting on space suits on this side and will burn our way through this jammed hatch, repair the damage and then pull you out. Now act quickly, or Yldra is lost!"

There was no answer from Ron.

"Hurry!" Yiddir exclaimed. "We can't burn through from here without causing the ice plug to melt in the hole, and without a space suit, Yldra would die—just like Gradon did in the execution chamber."

"Ron!" came Nad's voice.

Then Ron said, "I—I can't! The air will go out. I'll die!"

"Then die, you coward! If I find you alive and Yldra dead I'll kill you anyway!"

But Ron only fell in his chair and sobbed. "Kill me then!" he cried. "I can't do it! I love her, but I can't make myself do it!"

Nad and Yiddir were in space suits in the next chamber forward. Their forward hatch was sealed. Instead of using the heat gun, Nad blasted the hatch with a Disrupter and leaped into the room. But the ice plug cracked, and the air rushed out again. Before new ice could form, Yldra's nose and ears flowed red.

The two men carried her out to safety. Between them and Ron were two airless chambers.

Time passed endlessly for Ron, but nothing more happened. Finally, he addressed the sonophone in a choking voice.

"Nad!" he called. "Have you got her? Is she all right?"

After a long, terrible silence, Nad replied. "You don't know, do you?" he said. "Two airless rooms separate you from us, Ron. If you try to come out, you'll die. If you stay there, you'll suffocate in a few seconds. Just stay there and think about it!"

"Nad!" Ron called, frantically. "Tell me! Is she alive?"

"Your cowardice wrecked our plans before," came Nad's voice, murderously cold. *"Now what have you done to Yldra?"*

"Nad!" Ron was hysterical, crying out in falsetto. "Don't leave me here! Nad!"

But only silence answered him…

YLDRA died. Fortunately, Lylwani was spared the grief of the others, but Yiddir, Nad and Karg could only sit there in painful silence looking at her lovely form as it lay inert before them. All but Yiddir, perhaps, hoped that Ron would die in agony.

Silently, they prepared her for space burial, and just before they put her in the disposal lock, Nad bent over and kissed her cold forehead.

"Goodbye, sweet," he whispered, tenderly.

Ron, in a delirium of fright and mortal anguish, seemed to hear a distant voice chanting:

> *Oh Darkness that is Light!*
> *Oh mighty judge that offers peace*
> *forever in abysmal night!*
> *Oh Truth that gives me naked*
> *nothing for falsely vested life.*
> *Where in an instant that is ever*
> *I may be free of Wrong or Right!*

"Yldra!" he screamed. "Yldra!"

Silence brought loneliness to sit with his conscience, while the air about him grew stale…

YIDDIR finally prevailed upon Nad to rescue Ron. At first, Nad refused, with close-mouthed stubbornness, but when Karg offered to get in a space suit, Nad gave in.

They used one compartment for an air lock, and Nad went into the damaged chamber and repaired the holes. Then air was admitted and they announced to Ron over the sonophones that he could come out.

After almost a minute, the hatch opened, and Ron stood there looking blankly at his brother.

"Yldra is dead and buried in space," said Nad. "You didn't deserve to see her. If you care to live with yourself after this, I'm giving you your life back. Not that I can see why. You can thank Yiddir."

Ron's face was colorless, his eyes severely bloodshot, but the fear was gone out of him. In fact, the spirit had gone out of him.

They left him to his own resources for a while, but later on when it was necessary for him to speak, they found that he could not articulate. As though unseeing, he stared mutely through them. He ate and slept like a somnambulist.

"The shock may wear off in time," said Yiddir, sympathetically. "Nad, both you and Karg may despise Ron, but I feel terribly sorry for him. No man could experience a greater hell than to be born a coward and want to die and yet not have the courage to commit suicide. I know that Ron despises himself more, perhaps, than both of you put together. He is experiencing more punishment than anyone could possibly administer to him externally. Whether you may think so or not, I believe he loved Yldra as much as any man can love a woman, but the mechanism of cowardice worked in him in a way that was uncontrollable. Just leave him alone and give time a chance to heal his mind and shattered nerves."

After a long moment of silence in which neither Nad nor Karg could think of anything to say, Yiddir added, "We have more important things to worry about. That galactite damaged certain electrical circuits that are virtually inaccessible to us. Our meteor detection system works only intermittently. It can only be hoped that no meteors cross our path while the system is not functioning. Of course, the hull might withstand the blow, but the change of course might be violent and the inertia would most certainly kill us at this velocity. Just now the system is functioning again. I hope it continues to do so."

Yiddir looked significantly at Nad and felt that he was thinking of the same thing. If a meteor could get through without detection at some future date, so could Sargon.

THE great event they had been waiting for finally occurred. It happened one day when Nad was on watch and while Karg and Ron and Yiddir slept.

He was in the control room alone with Lylwani. Before him were control panels, and above these were large observation ports. There was nothing to do but watch the deceleration indicators occasionally.

Lylwani sat close beside Nad, looking blissfully at the black observation ports. Nad had been watching her affectionately. She appeared to be in good health, and the loneliness in him transformed her natural beauty into irresistible allure. He could not resist taking her hand in his and she did not object. In fact he was elated to feel the suggestion of a responsive pressure from her slender fingers.

She could converse and think for herself with a childlike simplicity, so Nad tried to engage her in conversation.

"You and I," he said, "are the last of our kind." There was no point in telling her of the arks, he thought.

"There is Yiddir," she replied, "and Karg, and Ron."

"I know, dearest, but—" He stopped, helplessly. How could he explain to an infant mind the pricelessness of their still extant ability to procreate their kind? How could he tell her that they were the potential parents of a new humanity?

"But what?" she asked, looking at him with the sweet, trusting mind of a child.

In her mind, he thought, she is a child, but physically she is a woman. She is *my* woman! He took her head between his hands, very gently, so as not to startle her.

"I must teach you to love me again," he said, "or I'll lose my mind."

"Love?" She raised her brows, quizzically.

"Yes," he said. "Love, Lylwani! A very important thing. Do you understand what it is to be happy?"

"I am happy."

"But I mean—happier."

"Very happy?"

"That's right, darling. When you love, you are very happy."

"I am very happy. Am I in love?"

A wave of discouragement sought to engulf him, but he persisted stubbornly.

"Do you know what this is?" he asked her, and then he kissed her gently while his arms ached to hold her.

She did not resist or respond, but he felt a slight tremor pass through her. Her eyes were wide, puzzled.

"Kiss?" she said.

"Kiss of love," he corrected. "Makes us both very happy. I love you, Lylwani. Do you love me?"

"Kiss," she said, raising her lips to his.

Nad swept her into his arms and kissed her as he had wanted to kiss her ever since they had left the ark, and she responded happily.

"You're mine, Lylwani...mine." he whispered.

"Mine," she answered, and her arms stole around his neck. "I am very happy."

WHEN Nad next looked up, something bothered him that he could not define. He started to turn back to Lylwani, but his attention was dragged back again to something—something that was not as it should be.

Then he saw, through the observation panel, several dim glimmerings of violet light. Lylwani felt his body tense and she arose from his arms.

"What is wrong?" she asked. Now Nad's cup was overflowing. A fierce, glad joy suffused him. "Look!" he cried, pointing at the lights. "The stars, Lylwani! *The stars!*"

"Stars?" She looked up in puzzlement at the lights. "I see lights—pretty lights."

"Oh don't worry about what they are sweetheart," he exclaimed. "They just make me very happy."

She frowned. "Happy? Do you love the stars?"

"I could kiss them…"

"I don't understand," she said. "Everything is love and kisses."

Nad laughed and hugged her. "Come on," he said. "Let's wake up the others and show them the stars!"

Yiddir and Karg came rushing forward when he called them, but Ron did not respond and they left him alone.

"Yes, there they are at last!" cried Yiddir, his old face flushed with the emotion of relief.

"Is that all they amount to?" queried Karg disappointedly. "I can see only about ten violet points of light."

"No," Yiddir laughed. "You see only the beginning of them. We have to slow down still more. We see only a few that are moving away from us, and their light waves are still reaching us at such a high frequency that we can only discern the highest visible band of their spectra. That is the so-called Doppler Effect. In a few hours you will see the blazing glory of God's whole universe…"

"This is a very happy occasion," said Karg.

"Are you happy?" Lylwani asked him.

"Yes," Karg answered. "Very happy."

To everyone's intense surprise, Lylwani kissed him. "The kiss of love will make you happier," she explained.

Karg blushed crimson and looked at Nad, who was utterly crestfallen. But the Martian's sense of humor saved the situation as he admonished Nad with mock severity.

"Teacher," he said, "you'll have to make your lessons more explicit!"

It was Nad's turn to blush. Both Yiddir and Karg patted him on the back with silent eloquence. They understood his problem.

"As soon as visibility has been completely established," Yiddir announced, in an effort to change the subject, "we're going to have a lot of work to do. I've got to locate definitely the solar system where our little planet is. It will be several weeks yet before we will be stationary and can start acceleration back toward our goal. Our trip to the planet will have to be made as much as possible within the speed of light, so it may take us a long time to reach it. Just how long I'll have to determine. If it is too many light years distant we'll have to plunge again into the velocity of darkness, but I hope not."

Yiddir thought of Ron. He reasoned that if Ron was mentally incapable of evaluating their present position it was a blessing. For otherwise his first thought must be, as was Yiddir's: *Poor Yldra died before she got to see the stars…*

CHAPTER EIGHT

TRUE to Yiddir's prediction, within a few hours the majority of the stars shifted into full spectrum visibility and shone with their natural light, at least to an effective extent. There was a slight tendency for the stars ahead to be predominantly blue-white and the ones astern to be predominantly yellow-white or even dull red, but Yiddir promised that within a week or so everything would be absolutely normal.

As the flaming universe took form before their eyes, they felt a great oppressiveness lift from them. Their spirits found room for expansion and life took on new values.

Ahead of them, in the direction of their goal, was a tremendous spectacle that none of them would ever forget. Towering in awe-inspiring grandeur among the great, blazing tiers and banks of stars was an opaque mass of gas that Yiddir said was hundreds of millions of kilometers in extent. He called it a nebula.

"Our little planet lies close beside it," he said, and he showed them a yellowish sun in the telescope that was the center of the system they sought. "The outer fringe of the dark nebula is at about the same distance as our planet," he explained. "It is about three light years away, so I am afraid we'll have to make a large part of tour journey in the darkness of higher velocity, but it will be necessary to watch our course and not get too close to the nebula."

"Why?" asked Karg, who was at the telescope.

A shadow of concern crossed momentarily over Yiddir's wrinkled brow. "I became informed, some time ago, of certain unaccountable phenomena connected with that region," he said. "Exploration reports are on file in the ark we have left, and I found the opportunity to peruse some of them secretly. At the time the rebel Navigators visited the little world we are seeking, several of the scout boats, such as this one, made numerous excursions to the nebula itself to gather samples of the gas for analysis. Their pilots and accompanying observers returned with accounts of strange physical phenomena occurring within the nebula. There were planes of strong gravitational currents separated by regions of no attraction whatsoever. One of the ships was almost lost in a powerful eddy for which they had no name but which I would call a space warp. My only theory on this subject is that the nebula is so huge and its gasses so dense that various regions of superior density have enough concentrated mass to set up strong gravitational fields. As these masses exert pressure, expand, contract, or attract each other, they cause motion as well, and probably a very complicated series of orbits is set up for multitudinous masses of gas, which change and change again. The result is that probably all the freak laws of Nature occur there and it would be dangerous for a ship to go too near to the nebula or to attempt to pass through it. That's why I want as much visual flight as I can get en route to the planet, because in the darkness of super velocity I could go off course and end up too close to that dark colossus."

Karg had been wandering among the star clusters with the telescope as Yiddir spoke. Now he turned and asked a question that brought Nad sharply to attention.

"Yiddir," he said. "I was present when you first contacted us by sonophone, and I remember you told us that Man had a magnificent purpose to accomplish in the living flesh. You said this purpose had been hidden from us by the Navigators who had robbed us of memory, and that you could not reveal it to us until we had learned many more facts. Is it the proper time now to ask you what that purpose is?"

At this point, Yiddir, alone, noticed that Ron focused his eyes on him, and that there glimmered in him the faintest spark of interest for the first time since Yldra's death.

"The answer to your question," he said, "is a very vital one, but also the most problematical one that may be asked. I can't answer you in one neat sentence. In fact, it may take me days, months, or even years to get the idea across to you, but if you'll be patient I'll start."

He then began to approach the subject of Man's duality, amazing them all with the concept of life beyond the flesh.

"Centuries and millennia ago, all this was so incomprehensible," he continued, "that it was discussed on the basis of a blind and trusting faith. As science developed in its constant search for the truth, certain things could not very readily be reconciled with the old religious ideas and they were regarded merely as parables disguising, for a more ignorant mass of people, the real truths that science was after. So atheism developed, unfortunately, and Man retrogressed through rank materialism almost to the brink of sheer animalism, until the scientists, still valiantly searching, finally found the road to a seeing and a *knowing* faith in Man's duality, by *proving* it, and by basing the new approach to godliness on the *proof* that nothing was supernatural—that even the next plane of existence was as physical as this. The discovery of sub-matter and second order phenomena led to the actual detection and even, in some cases, photographs, of Man's sub-material self. Just as in the flesh we are formed in embryo and born into the corporeal plane of existence, so the sub-material, or ethereal Man, or *spirit,* as it was once called, is embryonic within the living human, until our grosser body disintegrates and releases the final entity of Man into the sub-material world, which was once called Heaven, or the

Hereafter; but which we know now is merely a vast universe composed of a finer matter."

"But the purpose of our present existence—what is that?" asked Nad.

Yiddir smiled. "I could talk for years," he said, "but to make a long story short and go into the details later, I will tell you that there is one fundamental law behind all things, and failure to adhere to that law leads to disruption and unhappiness. That law says that there are two opposite forces—which may be called anything you like—active and passive, positive and negative, good and bad, construction and destruction. No matter where you look you find its manifestation: love and hate, man and woman, peace and war, happiness and despair. All is surge, or vibration between these opposites. Without surge and striving between these extremes there would be no energy, hence no matter, or space, or time, or existence. *And as Man is finite, so by this law may we positively deduce the Infinite Man*—called God; not an arbitrary entity sifting somewhere on an ethereal throne, but the Incomprehensible Total of all sub-material energy, of which we are part and contributors."

"But still I don't see the great purpose of life," protested Karg.

"That purpose," said Yiddir, "is expansion, surge, or striving toward godliness, *from finite to Infinite!* No civilization that defies this principle of Natural Law can progress or stabilize itself at all..."

"But how can we progress toward this godliness?" asked Nad.

"We are doing it now," said Yiddir. "In our self-denial and sacrifice to safeguard a potential future generation which must spring from you and Lylwani, we have advanced just that much out of our finite selves. Concentration upon self, alone, is merely a process of densifying and becoming infinitesimal even to the point of spiritual extinction."

At this point, Ron buried his face in his hands. And Yiddir knew, at last, that he had driven his point home.

IT required another week finally to eliminate their forward velocity. Yiddir handled the controls so expertly that they were without induced gravity for only a few seconds. Then acceleration took the plate of deceleration and they were on their way at last toward their distant goal.

In the meantime, Yiddir and Karg both took note of Nad's frequent use of the telescope. Instead of the expression of awe and wonderment that was always to be seen in Karg's face when he used the instrument, Nad's face reflected nothing but cold, grim determination. For hours, his narrowed, gray eyes searched the limitless vastness, and the other men knew he was not looking for new stars. At other times he watched the meteor detector, continually adjusting it for ultra-sensitivity, and yet they knew he was not trying to detect meteors. Then when the detection system failed momentarily owing to the intermittent short caused by the galactite, he would rush to the telescope and begin his vigil all over again.

Or at other times Nad would try to be alone with Lylwani, awakening her personality slowly and painstakingly to a more complete awareness of their situation. At last she was completely rational, requiring only the continued process of education and training to bring her back to her former self.

Ron, too, showed some slow signs of progress, although he was still inarticulate. Sometimes Yiddir found him, too, at the telescope, and he reflected that curiosity was a good sign of convalescence. He was even able to interest Ron in further training concerning space navigation.

Karg was all around handy man and dependable standby. He took complete charge of the converters and synthesized their food and water. Or at other times he would entertain them with his Martian *querla,* while Lylwani sang the songs he had taught her. Yiddir would sit silently meditating on the precarious future of a race of human beings that must originate from Nad and Lylwani—whom he considered in his mind as Adam and Eve.

Such was their state of affairs when ultra-velocity was approaching again and Yiddir prepared to hurl them into the darkness that lies beyond the speed of light. They were two and a half light years from their goal.

As the stars began to fade slowly from view, Nad suddenly demanded a decrease of speed, for the sake of visibility. He had been at the telescope several hours.

"What's the matter?" Yiddir asked him, and Karg and Lylwani crowded close to see.

Nad's eye was at the eyepiece and he was silent for almost a minute.

"I lost it," he said finally.

"Lost what?" Karg asked him.

Nad straightened up, his face slightly drawn with fatigue, and he brushed a mop of blond hair back from his forehead. "It might have been a meteor," he said, "and yet its velocity seemed to be too great."

Yiddir's eyes narrowed. "In which direction was it traveling?"

Nad answered his look, significantly. "It was moving parallel to us and at about the same speed."

"How far away?"

Nad shrugged. "Who can tell? The detectors can't pick it up."

Karg addressed both Yiddir and Nad, "You think it could be—"

"Sargon?" said Nad. "I don't know."

"Who is Sargon?" asked Lylwani.

Nad looked at her with deep affection. He put his arm around her and drew her close to him.

"I hope you never find out," he said.

That day their little ship hurled into the great darkness, an infinitesimal mote dwarfed into virtual nothingness by the towering enigma of the dark nebula.

NAD could not sleep. He lay in his bunk wide awake and tried to remember how long they had been traveling in the darkness of super velocity. Days? Weeks? Such units of time were almost without meaning in this terrible endlessness, and there was a year or a year and a half to go. Sometimes he had felt that the whole structure of his personality was going to slump suddenly into a shapeless puddle, because all the reasons that formed the props under his mental stability were but arbitrary synthesis, like the food that came out of the converters. But in such precarious moments he supported himself on two pillars of reality: his love for Lylwani and his hatred and suspicion of Sargon. Against his fear that Sargon might really be out there trailing them swiftly through the darkness was balanced the grim hope that he was there—that someday they would meet again and that he could rid himself of his bitterness by throttling his enemy forever.

Abandoning his attempt to rest, he finally got up and went forward to keep Karg company in the control room. When he arrived, however, he found the room empty. He looked at the instruments and found them steady. However, the pilot light over the meteor indicator was out again, as it had been of late with dangerous frequency.

Reasoning that Karg had gone to the observation bridge aft, he sat down idly at Yiddir's chart desk and puzzled over the star charts. Then he got up again and paced the room, a frown creasing his brow. Why was he so nervous? He tried to analyze himself. It was not just boredom. What was it?

Then he stopped dead still, eyes slowly widening with nameless apprehension. *What was wrong?*

The whole ship was too silent. He was accustomed to stillness out here in the void, but this was an absence of sound that pricked up the ears of instinct.

Swiftly, he went aft to look for Karg. The rear observation chamber was empty. He went to Yiddir's cabin and found him unconscious in his bunk, but as he shook him Yiddir slowly came to.

"I can't sleep," Yiddir mumbled, "been awake for hours."

"But you were unconscious!" said Nad. "You look like you've been knocked out. No color in your face at all!"

"You're rather pale, yourself," Yiddir replied, looking up at him curiously.

"Yiddir, something is wrong. I can't find Karg anywhere!"

The old man got up and accompanied Nad on a hasty tour of inspection. At last they found Karg. He was lying on the floor before the main hatch airlock, face down, a Disruptor clutched in one hand. His black hair was matted with blood.

Silently, both men bent over him and made a quick examination with a frenzied effort, Nad turned his friend over to look at his face. Yiddir lifted one of Karg's eyelids.

"He is dead," he commented. "Someone Stun Rayed him and then hit him over the head, Nad," he said, looking up gravely, "you and I were Stun Rayed while we slept."

Nad rose slowly, gathering a great breath into his lungs. Then he shouted, "Lylwani!" And he ran toward her cabin before Yiddir could advise him that her absence from the ship was the only possible deduction.

Weighted down by an awareness of ultimate tragedy, he sought the control room. The darkened pilot light over the meteor indicator confirmed his worst suspicions.

"She's gone! She's gone!" he heard Nad shouting to him.

Ron came reeling into the control room, his face white from the effects of the Stun Ray. In his eyes was one obvious question as he looked at Yiddir.

Yiddir replied, "Yes. It's happened. Sargon has struck at last, and Karg lost his life trying to oppose him."

Nad became ill with fever. For days he lay in his bunk, unable to eat or sleep, his eyes staring widely out of an ever thinning face. Sometimes he would talk or shout, as though in delirium. Yiddir doctored him as best he could, force feeding him at intervals, while he permitted the ship to hurtle onward through the darkness.

Ron's pale face remained absolutely expressionless, but a new purpose seemed to take hold of him. He, himself, manned the converters and took over most of Karg's old duties. At other times he would watch Yiddir for hours, mutely waiting for him to speak. There was no need to state the great question before them now. It was self-evident.

Without Lylwani, their expedition was futile, so why go on? Yet, why try to overtake either section of the fleet again? To what purpose? Was there a purpose at all?

Ron seemed to have a purpose, and he appeared to be waiting for Yiddir to perceive it and confirm its validity. But time passed. Many weeks passed, and Yiddir remained as inarticulate as Ron. Ron knew he was waiting for Nad to recover.

CHAPTER NINE

FINALLY, Nad did recover, but he appeared to have no will to live. When Yiddir thought he was strong enough, he at last voiced Ron's thoughts.

"There is only one thing we can do," he said. "We must establish our base on the small planet as planned. From there we will attempt to find the system or systems I am really looking for. Once we have found a real group of worthwhile planets and established photographic proof of their existence, we will use our converted drivers and try to overtake the Government Fleet. We will contact only Nor E-I-M, of the flagship. With our proofs, if we obtain what I think we are going to find, the fleet will turn back."

"I suppose you realize," said Nad, dully, "that it will take us a few more years at the least to acquire the proofs you want. By that time, to overtake either part of the fleet, even with your converted drive would occupy half a lifetime, if one survived madness and the increased danger of meteors."

"I admit that," said Yiddir. "But what else have we three to live for?"

"Nothing. Sheer blank, nothing."

"Then I suggest we adhere to the plan I have outlined."

"All right," Nad replied. "I hope we can all cling to our sanity in the meantime."

Ron got to his feet and limped over to the control board. He examined the instruments with renewed interest...

A YEAR of darkness passed, during which time Yiddir began again to decelerate. This time he conditioned himself and the others to withstand a slowly increased deceleration rate until they were living under a very abnormal induced gravity. His object was to emerge from the velocity of darkness soon enough to leave a safe margin between them and the dark nebula.

But before they had quite emerged from the darkness, their meteor shield failed them once more, and this time a small meteor struck them squarely. The cryosite hull took the blow, but inertia resulting from their slight change of course came near to killing them. From that day forward, Yiddir's health began to wane as the result of internal injuries.

Furthermore, it was discovered that as a result of the collision with the meteor the controls to the drivers were severed, and all they had left were their decelerators.

"It will be necessary for one of us to go outside in a space suit and inspect the damage to see if it can be repaired," Yiddir said. "I believe I am physically incapable of going out there, and Ron's bad foot may hinder him seriously. Moreover, I am not sure that he would be able to learn quickly enough what I'd have to teach him. Even if I did teach him, he would no doubt be terrorized by the experience. I'm afraid you're the only one who could do the job, Nad. We still have several months' time while we decelerate, but by that time those controls should be repaired, or I'm afraid I won't be able to bring us safely in to our planet. I'll have to begin instructing you at once concerning what you're going to have to look for and possibly repair."

There was nothing else to be done. For seemingly endless weeks Yiddir instructed Nad, while Ron took over almost all the duties on board. In the meantime the stars reappeared and the dark nebula was apparently so close that it formed one side of the whole universe. The sun of the one planet solar system they sought was still a star, but of the brightest magnitude in their region of space. In the telescope they could discern the tiny pinpoint of light that was their planet, but only for a short period of time while it was in full phase.

The chief problem was to decelerate fast enough to escape falling within the inimical influence of the nebula. Yet in Yiddir's condition no greater deceleration could be endured. In fact, Nad secretly decreased the deceleration rate sometimes when Yiddir fainted or dropped into fitful sleep. Inevitably, they came closer to the nebula than they had intended. Ron knew what was happening, because he had been a witness to Nad's special adjustment of these controls. Strangely, he showed no fear of the consequences. He was Nad's silent companion in all things now.

One day when Yiddir felt well enough to make observations he became greatly alarmed by their position. Already, some portions of the universe that had been plainly visible before were turning dim because they had penetrated the attenuated outer limits of the nebula.

"Nad, we can wait no longer," he said. "You've got to go outside and see what you can do about those driver controls. Our course must be changed quickly or we will be at grips with unpredictable fields and extremes of gravity that may do us great harm or cause us to become lost irretrievably within the nebula."

So Nad donned his suit, picked up his tools and instruments, and entered the main airlock, while Ron stood tensely by, watching with widened eyes. But again Nad knew this was not fear. It was apprehension for his own safety. He waved at his brother reassuringly just as the outer door opened, exposing him to the vast Abyss. The rush of air out of the lock would have carried him into emptiness if it had not been for his magnetic traction produced by his shoes. Only then did he suddenly realize how alone he really was.

Before him, endless space yawned apathetically, coldly, and silence greater than he had ever known gripped him like the hand of Death. In spite of the grip maintained by his magnetic shoes, he had to struggle with giddiness and instinctive terror. Under Yiddir's guidance over the sonophone extension that he dragged behind him, he moved aft along the dimly glistening hull, like a deep-sea diver in a bottomless ocean.

For two hours, Nad worked in the damaged area of the drivers, relaying his observations to Yiddir. He cut open hard cryosite channels to get at control conduits, bridged damaged gaps with his instruments and waited for Yiddir's readings from the control panels inside.

Three times, Nad had to enter the ship and return to the outside, and thus another day passed, while they penetrated deeper into the nebula, and the stars became almost lost to sight. But now he was outside for the last time. This time he was finishing the job.

When Yiddir gave a cry of triumph and the drivers spit out a lightning blast in response to his controls, Nad knew his precarious work was done and he stood up, preparing to enter the ship again.

RON had entered a small observation dome in the center of the ship in an effort to watch Nad. From his position he could make out the dim outlines of the aft driver nacelles, and there he saw his brother trying to collect his tools, preparatory to re-entering the ship.

At that moment, a slight attenuation in the nebulous gas outside enabled Ron to discern something that was utterly incredible to him. Briefly he saw it, a great, shadowy outline that stood out clearly for one moment and then was gone again. *A ship!* A ship exactly like their own, drifting helplessly in the nebula!

Then he saw it again, this time much nearer. He could see its forward observation port, ablaze now with light, and a woman's face appeared behind it, peering out at him.

"Lylwani!" he thought, his mind reeling with astonishment.

But he was given little time for speculation, because in the same instant he saw a grotesque figure move on the exterior of the other ship's hull. Sargon, too, had come outside to affect repairs.

Just as the ships drifted within the influence of their mutual attraction, Nad straightened up and faced Sargon. Ron knew they were looking at each other and waiting for the two ships to come together. He also knew that Nad could not help seeing something else, something which must have made him go insane with rage and anguish. For just in the last brief moment of visibility, Lylwani could be seen very plainly in the observation port. In her arms was an infant child.

Ron saw both space-suited figures lunge toward each other, each with a blinding white cryosite torch in his hand, and then the curtain of the nebula suddenly engulfed the scene.

SUDDENLY, Ron darted forward as fast as his club foot would allow, and he was just in time to stay Yiddir's hand at the controls. If the drivers had been activated, the other ship might have been lost forever, and if Nad had stepped across to it they would have lost him, also.

Yiddir had felt the impact of the other vessel, but as he could not see it from his location he had no idea what it was. Then, to his wonderment, Ron momentarily found his voice.

"S—Sargon!" he said, hoarsely, with an almost superhuman effort.

"*Sargon!*" Yiddir's old eyes blazed with alarm.

Speech failing him again, Ron went through a frantic pantomime to show how the two vessels had come together and how Nad and Sargon had charged each other in mortal combat.

Hastily, Yiddir went to the central observation blister and tried to observe what was happening. But now the dark gases were too dense. He could occasionally discern the shadowy outline of the other hull, plus a dim glow of light from the other observation port, but he could see nothing else. In fact, even that faded out as the two ships were carried into regions of maximum density.

He and Ron could only sit there and wait, well aware of the long pent-up emotions that were being unleashed out there in that precarious darkness. At any moment the nebula could throw them into a new spin and lose the other ship forever.

Yiddir asked Ron if he had seen any sign of Lylwani, and Ron nodded assent. He made a cradle of his arms and moved them back and forth, significantly.

"What!" Yiddir exclaimed. "She has a child?"

Again, Ron nodded affirmatively. Yiddir reflected that more than a year had passed since Lylwani's abduction. Terror gripped his heart to think that she and the infant were so close in this infinite emptiness and that one lurch of the ship could lose them forever. His heart was with Nad, too, in his understanding of what his emotions must be. He could not begrudge him the rage and anguish that had hurled him against Sargon.

But what of the outcome? Suppose Sargon should win?

Just then there came to their ears the muffled sound of air compressors, and both of them knew that someone had entered the airlock. They ran to it without weighing the possible consequences.

There in the lock was a figure in a space-suit, but they could not tell whether it was Nad or Sargon. As they watched, the figure dragged in behind it another figure clad in a space-suit, and both observers felt their pulse surge with a new hope. This was either Sargon dragging Nad, or Nad dragging Sargon, and in either case they knew that Nad was still with them.

Hastily, Yiddir activated the valves and the outer door closed while air shot back into the lock. The figure outside opened the inner door before Yiddir could perform the service for him. At the same time, the standing figure helped the prone figure to its feet. Then the first figure opened its faceplate, and Sargon spoke to them, peremptorily.

"Help me with this suit, quick!" Whereupon he started to dismantle the other figure's suit. Yiddir unscrewed the helmet and lifted it hastily, expecting to find Nad.

But there before him was the pale face of Lylwani! And he and Ron observed again in her eyes the childishness of a victim of the M-Ray.

"Baby!" she gasped, as she struggled in the depths of her suit, and Yiddir was alarmed to hear the muffled scream of an infant.

When he stripped off the top section, the small child came to light, its face almost blue from partial asphyxiation.

Ron helped Lylwani to a seat, while Yiddir stood there trying to contain himself. His mind staggered under the impact of the realization of what Sargon had done. Jealous of Lylwani's newly acquired memory of Nad and love for him, Sargon had subjected her to the M-Ray, and then he had forced her to be his mate.

He turned on Sargon, his face red with rage. "You dirty, foul beast of Satan!" he exclaimed.

In their distraction with Lylwani and the child they had not seen Sargon extract an M-Ray from his spacesuit. He was half out of it now, and he stood there looking at them with a menacing scowl.

"You might as well take it this way," he said. "We're all in this together, and if we want to survive we'll have to work together. I've been struggling with a disabled ship for months. Now it's gone to God knows where in the nebula. It jerked loose just as I brought Lylwani over."

"But what happened to Nad?" asked Yiddir. "Did you kill him and leave him outside?"

"Neither one," replied Sargon, the shadow of a grim smile on his lips. "He lost pretty much air when I cracked his faceplate, but I think he'll live, because I brought him inside."

"Inside!" Yiddir's eyes widened in horror, incredulous. "Inside *what?*"

"Inside the other ship."

"You mean—" Yiddir staggered, fighting to keep from passing out.

"Yes," snarled Sargon. "In the other ship out there lost in the nebula. If he manages to recover, he'll find himself in a disabled ship, fully capable of supplying him with all the food and water and air he needs—but a drifting derelict."

"But, good God! He'll go mad!"

"It's less than he deserves," Sargon replied, divesting himself of the rest of his suit. "It's just the way I wanted it. Killing was too good for him. I think he saw Lylwani and the child. I want him to spend a lot of time in absolute loneliness thinking about that. I hope he never goes mad. I hope he spends his whole life thinking about it..."

Just as Yiddir dropped to the floor, overcome by shock in his weakened condition, Ron lunged at Sargon's legs and bore him to the floor. In a blind frenzy of hate, he sought the Martian's throat. But Sargon landed a mighty rabbit punch on the back of his neck and he slumped into unconsciousness.

IT WAS Sargon who piloted the ship out of the nebula and plotted a straight course to the planet. When Yiddir felt better, Sargon had a talk with him.

"When my ship became disabled," he said, "I had to abandon my original plans for returning to the fleet. I figured that if I could make it to the planet I was lucky. Well, I couldn't make repairs in time to keep from tangling with the nebula, and I had about given up hope when I drifted into you. *That* was just unheard of luck! Wouldn't have happened again in a million years."

"Sargon," said Yiddir, bitterly, "do you think that you will ever be able to really enjoy life again, knowing what you've done with Nad? You condemned him to that terrible fate at a time when your emotions were governing your reasoning, but later on, in your more sober moments of reflection, you may be haunted by the vision of him, a lonely madman drifting helplessly in the nebula."

Sargon scowled. "He can always open the airlock," he said. "I'd do it. It's the easy way out. Besides, he may be dead anyway. He was out cold when I left him.

"But that's all behind us now. What I'm concerned with is the future. To return to either section of the fleet, even with your converted drive, would take years. If it were just straight distance to cover we could make it much sooner, but both fleets are moving, too, much faster than light. Well, I've thought it all over a lot of times. I've weighed my possible rewards and advantages to be derived from returning to the arks against the terrible years of waiting through such a long journey. It's not worth it, so it looks like the planet is the answer."

Yiddir then carefully outlined his own ideas concerning further exploration. He emphasized the importance of notifying the Government Fleet, at any sacrifice, in the event such a discovery could be made.

"I am quite sure I have not long to live," he continued. "So you will have to do it, Sargon. As a member of the human race, it is your duty to do it. Your own rebel section of the fleet might conceivably come back and try to invade any planets colonized by Government forces, and whether they might succeed in taking over or not would make little difference. What matters is the people. They must be given a chance. Once installed in a suitable natural environment, I have complete confidence that our species can outlive any form of dictatorial rule that can be imposed upon it. That has always been borne out to be true in the past and I don't see why it shouldn't be true in the future."

"That's neither here nor there," replied Sargon impatiently. "As far as your idea about a better solar system is concerned, I think that's a little imaginative. I was a first hand witness to previous explorations in this region, you know, and I can tell you there's nothing out here but this one little planet. I'm not going to spend my time—"

Yiddir's eyes flashed indignantly. "Sargon," he interrupted, "have you any idea of who I really am?"

"Yes, I know. Yiddir E-5I7 2-P was an alias."

"And my real name is?"

"Korlon E-3-N. All right, so you used to be captain of the ark. But that was many years ago, and—"

"I was also something else!"

"So you were a famous scientist, too. But that's not—"

Yiddir sat up in his bunk and grasped Sargon's powerful arm. "Don't you realize," he argued, "that I was, even at the time of your exploration of this region, the most qualified astro-physicist on board? I had my own equipment, which I had improved over your own. I *know* what I'm saying when I tell you there are other suns in this region which are favorable to our existence!"

"Suns, maybe, yes, but not planets. We've looked, and there aren't any more."

"Then let Ron go exploring, after you've settled. Promise me you'll do at least that."

Sargon laughed. *"That* coward! What could he do but shake to pieces with fright at the mere thought of being left alone in a space ship."

Yiddir was too weak to argue further. But as the ship drew nearer to the small planet and he lay helplessly in his bunk, he was not at a loss for subjects upon which to meditate through the long hours.

CHAPTER TEN

WHEN the planet acquired a visible disk, Ron and even Lylwani became interested, although the latter was merely attracted to it because of its beautiful color and changing aspect. To Ron, however, it was fascinating because he knew how rare this planet was. He knew that it was on such a world that his ancestors had been born. As he observed its atmosphere, glowing like a silvery halo in the telescope, and as he saw its green jungles and smoldering young mountains and steaming oceans, he would often think of Yldra, who might have been there at his side, looking at all this for the first time. And then he would rescue his mind from vertigo by thinking of something outside the sphere of his personal emotions. The Government Fleet…he strove to keep his mind on that. The fleet, with its hundreds of thousands of people, moving outward, ever outward into vastness, searching vainly for a new home, for a natural way of life, for a means of survival…

Sargon affected a safe landing on a wild stretch of beach beside a primitive sea. Towering carboniferous forests loomed above them, and the bright sun shone hotly through a humid atmosphere. Gravitation was light, however, and it was a tremendous relief to everyone to be freed from the oppressive burden of deceleration. Even Yiddir felt well enough to give Sargon some assistance with the scientific problems connected with their emergence into this primitive world.

Air, water, solar radiations, samples of soil, fauna and flora—all had to be analyzed carefully. If Yiddir had not been able to help Sargon, certain mistakes might have been made which would have resulted in an early death for all of them. Very fortunately for them, the spaceship's cosmic energy converters were in good working condition, and they lived by synthesis as usual.

Inasmuch as the ship, designed to house a hundred Passengers, was roomy, self-sufficient, and impervious to the influences of their surroundings, Sargon could see no reason for building permanently on the ground. This was disappointing to Yiddir, because as long as Sargon and Lylwani and the child, Dirno, required the ship for a home, the possibilities of using it for further explorations were reduced proportionately. He had no hope of being able to make the exploratory trips himself, because he was virtually an invalid now. He tried occasionally to prevail upon Sargon to make an attempt to find the better solar system he knew existed in that region, but as Sargon procrastinated and time passed, the old man was finally forced to give up all hope of finding reasons for contacting either portion of the fleet. Here he would certainly die, and the little generation of brothers and sisters to be produced by Sargon and Lylwani would have to establish a new humanity here. In the meantime, Ron waited in silence—for what, no one knew, but he gave everybody the impression of patient waiting.

A year passed, not without some progress. They explored and mapped most of the planet by air. They also found a new base, on a plateau overlooking a broad inland sea of fresh water. Here the jungle was less aggressive and the forms of animal life were less carnivorous and destructive. They could go about without space suits at last, and the change and outdoor exercise worked a great improvement on all of them except Yiddir, who was the victim of recurrent hemorrhages as a result of his old injuries.

Sargon had even begun to take interest in establishing a permanent base on the ground. He learned how to use lumber. When he needed other materials, such as metal, he had only to synthesize it in the converters. Base metallic stock could be melted, cast, forged, and machined. In time, the foundations of a large building began to take shape, with Ron's willing assistance. Lylwani busied herself quite happily with her small son, Dirno, while Yiddir sat often in the mild sunlight of late afternoons and watched her in unhappy reflection. He thought of another man whose companionship might have enriched her life a hundredfold. And then he would sigh and wish for death to overtake him…

ONE day when all of them were eating together in the ship, Lylwani made a statement so startling that no one took another bite after she spoke. As she had done during her previous period of recovery from the M-Ray, she had also progressed this time to the point where she could think independently, at least as a child, and hold a simple conversation. As they sat discussing the small events of the day, some mention was made of Yiddir's long white beard and Sargon's bushy black one.

"But I like gold colored beards best," she said, without preamble. She continued eating as though she had made the most casual remark in the world.

Sargon reacted first, perhaps ten seconds sooner than Yiddir or Ron. He lowered his fork and spoke to her.

"Where did you ever see such a heard?" he asked.

She looked up and smiled sweetly at him. "The man in the forest has one," she said, innocently.

Sargon looked at Yiddir and saw his own thoughts reflected in the other's faded eyes. He got to his feet.

"*What* man in the forest?"

Lylwani looked up, raising her eyebrows in surprise. "Oh, he's a very wonderful man," she said. "He is so kind to me and Dirno. He has such strange eyes, and his hair and beard are all made of gold."

Sargon walked around the table and grasped her by the arm. "Where did you see this man?" he demanded.

Lylwani began to cry. She disliked and could never understand Sargon's roughness.

"Just a minute," Yiddir interrupted. "If you want any information, leave her to me. You'll get nothing out of her by frightening her."

Sargon knew that Lylwani was very fond of Yiddir. In any other circumstance he would have bullied her, jealously asserting his assumed prerogatives as father of her child, but now he gave in and stepped aside. He sat down at the table again and watched her intently as Yiddir questioned her and Ron watched the proceedings and listened with a pale, tense look of desperation.

"Lylwani," said Yiddir, gently.

"Please help us. We want to know your man with the golden beard, too. He must be a very wonderful sight. Won't you tell us more about him?"

Finally, Lylwani complied. She related how he had first contacted her several weeks before. Ron had built a little summer house for her and the child, where she could rest and enjoy the fresh air and be shielded from the hot sunlight. It was some distance removed from the ship, but in plain view, except that it blocked from view a patch of jungle immediately behind it.

One day, she told them, the golden bearded man had come to her from the jungle. He had called her by her name and spoken very nicely to her and played with Dirno. Then, when Sargon had approached the place, he had seemed angry and had gone back into the jungle. Three times he had come to see her. Yes, she confirmed, he had worn clothing, but it was very ragged, and he carried no weapons with him.

"He shouldn't be afraid of us, should he?" she asked. "Why can't we invite him to stay with us?"

"Man! Man!" gurgled Dirno, happily.

"You see," Lylwani smiled. "Dirno knows who we mean. He wants him, too. Why don't you bring him here?"

"Yes," said Sargon, with a mirthless grin. "I think we should bring the man here..."

THAT afternoon and all the next day Sargon roamed the jungle with two Disruptors, but he did not go too far astray. Frequently he would seek out a place where he could look back at the plateau where the ship was. Then he would stalk his intended quarry again.

Finally, hunger drove him back to the ship that night. He was surprised to find that Ron was absent, because Ron had evidenced a marked fear of the forest with its mysterious denizens. When Ron finally returned, he gave every evidence, by his extreme exhaustion and torn clothing, of having been on the same quest all day. In his hand he carried a Stun Ray. Sargon's eyes narrowed, but he said nothing. There was no necessity for anyone to say anything. It was tacitly understood that a simple sort of primordial law had set in, and the outcome of each individual's efforts now was in the hands of fate. The stakes were grimly vital.

The next morning, however, Ron could not find his Stun Ray. In the whole ship neither he nor Yiddir could find a single hand weapon.

"Sargon must have concealed them last night," said Yiddir at last.

For answer, Ron started off empty handed toward the jungle.

"Ron!" Yiddir called, helpless to follow. "Come back!"

But Ron did not stop, and soon his limping figure was lost to view in the deep shadow of the towering trees.

"Are they looking for the golden man?" asked Lylwani, innocently.

Yiddir put his arm around her, affectionately. "Yes, Lylwani," he answered.

"Oh I hope they find him. I hope he comes back again," she said.

"Yes, I hope *he* comes back…"

CHAPTER ELEVEN

BY noon that day, Sargon discovered the other ship. There was every sign that its pilot had taken great pains to conceal it. It lay in a deep gulley, half covered with fallen vines and trees that had been burned down with the ship's Disruptor cannons.

Without the slightest hesitation, Sargon set his Disruptors to maximum and fired at the ship. Time after time he fired, while explosions rocked the ground and the ship became a white inferno of dissolution.

Then he ran, fearing that he might have failed to destroy one or more of the reactors. Disrupted by the heat and explosions, unbalanced reaction might set in and they would blow, which was what he really wanted. A full atomic blast would clean out the last vestige of this thing he hated, and perhaps its pilot as well, if he were lurking somewhere within half a mile.

Eyes wide with the excitement of mingled triumph and awareness of mortal danger, he ran through the jungle like a madman. Once he dropped a Disruptor and it fell between mighty tree roots into some recess that he could not reach. There was no time to look for it. He ran onward, never daring to stop.

When he had traversed a good mile and a half of the jungle, the reactors blew. In one brief instant everything stood out in blinding contrast, illuminated by a flash of intense light that came near to blinding him. Then came a sound that he felt more than heard because he was momentarily deafened by it. He groveled under a great fallen log as the shock wave followed.

Giant trees crashed all about him and debris flew with the velocity of a hurricane. The jungle life set up one huge din, a roar and shrieking and bleating of abject terror.

He got to his feet and ran again, stumbling and picking himself up and running again, to get out of the area that he knew would soon be blighted by radioactive dust.

Close to the clearing where his own ship lay, he stumbled again, momentarily losing his grip on his one remaining Disruptor. As he lay there, panting, looking at the deadly weapon just three feet from him, he heard a crashing in the underbrush ahead. Then there stepped into his view, not twenty feet away, a man with golden blond hair and a year's growth of blond beard. A pair of gray eyes looked at him out of shadows that had never been there before—shadows of terror and near madness, filled with haunting memories of secret things that no other man had ever seen. It seemed to Sargon in that moment that this unarmed, half naked mortal enemy of his was looking at him from out of the grave. His body was full and hardened, in apparently excellent condition, but it was the look in his eyes that made Sargon lunge toward his Disruptor.

Just then a body hurtled over his head and Ron fell flat on the Disruptor, clutching it so tightly in his arms that Sargon could not dislodge him in time. He sprang to his feet just in time to receive a blow from the bearded one that sent him staggering off balance into the bushes.

When he could see clearly again, he saw Ron hand the Disruptor to Nad. Nad only stood there looking at Sargon with his death-haunted eyes, while Sargon's flesh crept and he sweated.

"You left me without weapons," said Nad, in a toneless voice. "Even if I had chosen suicide—which I did *not!*" His gray eyes blazed. "I could only have chosen the Abyss. That's the way you wanted it, wasn't it? There are no weapons at your ship, either. You seem to enjoy holding all the cards, don't you, Sargon?"

A deathly stillness ensued, while Nad just stood there looking at him.

"How—how did you—" Sargon stammered.

"How did I survive?" Nad finished the sentence for him. "How did I repair the ship? Thanks to Yiddir's patient instructions, I knew more about what was wrong than you did. But a lot has happened since then. Before emerging from the nebula I was drawn to its center, where I made an amazing discovery, thanks to you. I found—" He paused, looking at Sargon with cold deliberation. "But you're never going to see it, so why should I tell you? Get on your feet!"

Sargon scrambled to his feet. "All right, you've won!" he shouted, white with fear. "Take everything. Take the ship. Take Lylwani and Dirno, but don't shoot me in cold blood!"

Suddenly, Nad looked down at the Disruptor as though he had forgotten it was in his hands. Then, to Ron's amazement, he threw it away with all his might, and it became lost in impenetrable undergrowth.

"This is what I have waited for—and dreamed of—during all the time I spent—out there." He started toward Sargon. "I've got to do it with my bare hands!" he yelled, and he charged.

Sargon's confidence returned when he saw the Disruptor fly over the bushes, and in the same instant he knew this was what he wanted, too. With a fierce shout of triumph, he met Nad's charge...

Ron stood motionlessly to one side, watching them. He knew that this was inevitable. He also knew, somehow, that Nad preferred to die rather than accept outside help, even if Ron had been able to give it. Nor was it a matter of principle, it was a life-consuming hate that could only be expended in one way. Ron knew he had to leave both of them alone. He knew that if Sargon killed Nad he would have to stand there and watch him die.

As he watched, what he witnessed sickened him so that he felt faint. His legs failed him and he sat down. He did not know how two human bodies could take such punishment and still keep on struggling. The towering, pristine jungle held them as though in its lap, like some primitive god, understanding its children who obeyed the earliest law ever written—that which rules all the forces of construction and destruction, of love and hate, of survival and, death...

It lasted about fifteen minutes. Nad dragged himself, somehow, off of Sargon's prostrate body and stood up. He groped, as one blind, took two steps, and then fell on his face. Ron struggled with him and finally got him on his feet again. As he left the small clearing, he looked back at Sargon and shuddered. There was no doubt that Sargon was absolutely dead...

SO it was that Nad returned out of virtual limbo. He and Ron and Yiddir, with Lylwani and the small son of Sargon, left the small planet behind them—a planet that was still too young to receive them and too small to support the potential expansion of a new human race.

Nad piloted the ship back to the nebula and plunged directly into its weird darkness. He refused to tell even Yiddir what he had found, except to say that it was definitely the end of their search. There was a tense time of waiting, during which they struggled with the freak gravitational fields and ether warps within the nebula.

Then, suddenly, they burst into the tremendous interior, and Yiddir's heart leapt in exultation. For there it was, the solar system he had detected—a more spectacular and beautiful system than he could have imagined in his most optimistic dreams. Ron and Lylwani joined him in wonderment and awe.

Four white suns filled that tremendous chamber with a light that was sheer heavenly splendor. They formed the center of a system that possessed at least eight major planets, five minor ones, and a decorative host of thousands of planetoids and satellites. None of them showed distinct phases, because the sunlight seemed to be everywhere. On the "night side" of the various planets there was only a silvery twilight.

The world Nad had chosen was the fourth minor planet. It was roughly nine thousand miles in diameter and possessed about one-sixth land area and five-sixths water area. Yiddir knew even before he analyzed it that the atmosphere was healthful.

They landed by a broad river, just above a great waterfall, on a plateau that overlooked green jungle and a broad, blue ocean. At that altitude, the jungle had given way to mighty forests of coniferous trees, interspersed with great, rolling green prairie-lands that swept gently away and upward to snow-capped mountains.

"This is Paradise," said Yiddir. "Thank God I've lived to see it!"

TWO years passed, during which Yiddir's life faded slowly away and new life took his place, for to Lylwani was born a baby girl, whom they named Yldra. The boy, Dirno, and his step-sister, Yldra, throve in their healthful environment as though their race had been indigenous to it. Lylwani made rapid recovery and happily accepted Nad as her man, forever.

Ron seemed to be the only one who was not content to adjust himself. He worked harder than anyone else to establish a permanent base on the ground. A sturdy house of wood and steel took shape. Storehouses, workshops and sheds followed. Out of the ship's converters came metal, which was processed, forged and machined—under Yiddir's occasional supervision. New hand weapons were made, and the Disruptor cannons were transferred to permanent installations on the ground, as a source of nuclear energy. And at last certain plants and animals were domesticated. The foundation for a natural adjustment to the new world was finally set.

It was when Yiddir finally lay on his death bed that his ultimate wish was expressed.

"Your little beginning here," he said to Nad and Lylwani, "will require a millennium to bear substantial fruit. I regret very much that neither part of our divided fleet may ever know of this paradise you have discovered. By now the rebel fleet should be more than half way to its goal, and there is no one who can turn their course to this place. I wish they might be turned back before they invade those other planets. Even if they are rebels, all, the Passengers should certainly be considered. They should be given a chance. Dictatorial governments come and go, but humanity goes on forever.

"Still, if there was a choice to be made, I'd prefer to notify the Fleet Government. The rebels have some sort of chance on those other worlds, if they survive the conflict, but the other arks are only plunging ever more deeply into the Unknown. I can understand why it is impossible for you, Nad, to go. It would take more than half a lifetime to catch up with them now, even with the converted drivers. Still, it is sad to think that Dirno and Yldra, your children, will find themselves alone in this great solar system after you are gone."

Yiddir's dimming eyes did not fail to notice that Ron was standing in the background, listening intently. "If you ever could contact the Government Fleet," he said, "it would be worth more than life, itself. I'd try to locate Nor E-I-M, because he is the only person I can think of who might possibly be able to defend this place against the rebels, should they ever come back here exploring. There are some among their number who suspected the existence of this place more than they cared to admit to their companions."

Nad thought silently for a long while, and Yiddir smiled inwardly when he observed that Ron had disappeared.

"I could leave Ron with Lylwani," Nad said, finally.

Yiddir laid his withered hand on his arm. "It would take years, Nad—years. Your children would both be grown to adulthood before you reached the arks."

A ripple of muscles appeared along Nad's jaws. "But it must be done!" he exclaimed.

Just then, he heard a roar of rockets outside, accompanied by an unmistakable *swoosh!* He tried to jump to his feet, but Yiddir held him.

"Relax, Nad," said Yiddir. "I knew it was going to happen. This is what he has been waiting for. It took great courage, but he has found that in full measure at last."

Nad glared at him. "What do you mean?"

"Ron," said Yiddir, with his last breath, "has gone to find Nor—to bring back the Government Fleet. A poor, misguided coward with a club foot, who fought his cowardice and failed, only to lose Yldra, whom he loved perhaps in a way and with a depth of feeling which we could never understand. And finally the shock of that loss has made of him such a hero that his name may shine through all the pages of Man's future history—if he—succeeds..."

WHEN Dirno was seventeen years old, Nad and Lylwani had almost forgotten the strange and all but hopeless mission of Ron. There were three more children, two boys and a girl. All the elements of their natural environment had combined to assist their adaptation to normal life, and their parents found the afternoon of their existence to be the fulfillment of human desire—except for infrequently recurrent memories that sometimes haunted Nad in his deeper moments of reflection.

Sometimes in the still hours of the night when Lylwani lay sleeping beside him, his mind would still wander out beyond the stupendous, black walls of the nebula and try to find his lost brother, Ron. He would quail at the thought of the other's loneliness, riding the star-roads outward toward the edge of the galaxy, searching for an invisible fleet. Logic told him that Ron had failed, that in using the ultra-velocity available from the converted drivers he had made himself the victim of meteors—or that a lifetime of terrible loneliness had robbed him at last of his sanity. Sometimes he would dream that Ron was a white-haired maniac, whose star-blinded eyes stared at him from afar out of the Abyss, and he would awake with a start...

NOR E-I-M was a man in his early seventies, still straight of limb and of an alert, military manner. His distinguishing mane of gray hair was vigorous and thick, and his blue eyes reflected a brightness of mind that had defied the years. For one week he and his medical staff had worked on the stranger from the Abyss. Under special second-order-type rays of his own devising, he had thrown the man's conscious mind into a restful coma, and his nervous system was subjected to a complete re-energizing process. When they brought him back to consciousness, he was able to talk, haltingly, but effectively. He told them of a hidden paradise lying within the depths of the dark nebula, and of Yiddir and Nad and Sargon and Lylwani and the children and the rebel fleet.

"Of course you may think me insane," said Ron, wearily.

"On the contrary," Nor smiled. "I know this Yiddir of whom you speak, and I am quite sure the discovery you mention was actually made. In fact, we are going to return to the nebula. We may require another generation of time to reach it, but we will get there. If the rebel fleet has returned there and established a dictatorial government, we will overcome that government..."

"But they have the M-Ray," Ron reminded him.

"And I have, at long last, finally perfected an effective screen against it—plus a lot more," Nor told him, calmly.

"You...!" Ron's eyes widened. "But only Yiddir's son—"

Nor smiled again. "This Yiddir you speak of," he said, "was in reality Korlon E-3-N. I know, because he was my father..."

THE END

If you've enjoyed this book, you will not want to miss these terrific titles...

ARMCHAIR SCI-FI & HORROR DOUBLE NOVELS, $12.95 each

D-131   **COSMIC KILL** by Robert Silverberg
BEYOND THE END OF SPACE by John W. Campbell

D-132   **THE DARK OTHER** by Stanley Weinbaum)
WITCH OF THE DEMON SEAS by Poul Anderson

D-133   **PLANET OF THE SMALL MEN** by Murray Leinster
MASTERS OF SPACE by E. E. "Doc" Smith & E. Everett Evans

D-134   **BEFORE THE ASTEROIDS** by Harl Vincent
SIXTH GLACIER, THE by Marius

D-135   **AFTER WORLD'S END** by Jack Williamson
THE FLOATING ROBOT by David Wright O'Brien

D-136   **NINE WORLDS WEST** by Paul W. Fairman
FRONTIERS BEYOND THE SUN by Rog Phillips

D-137   **THE COSMIC KINGS** by Edmond Hamilton
LONE STAR PLANET by H. Beam Piper & John J. McGuire

D-138   **BEYOND THE DARKNESS** by S. J. Byrne
THE FIRELESS AGE by David H. Keller, M. D.

D-139   **FLAME JEWEL OF THE ANCIENTS** by Edwin L. Graber
THE PIRATE PLANET by Charles W. Diffin

D-140   **ADDRESS: CENTAURI** by F. L. Wallace
IF THESE BE GODS by Algis Budrys

ARMCHAIR SCIENCE FICTION & HORROR CLASSICS, $12.95 each

C-58   **THE WITCHING NIGHT**
by Leslie Waller

C-59   **SEARCH THE SKY**
by Frederick Pohl and C. M. Kornbluth

C-60   **INTRIGUE ON THE UPPER LEVEL**
by Thomas Temple Hoyne

ARMCHAIR SCI-FI & HORROR GEMS SERIES, $12.95 each

G-15   **SCIENCE FICTION GEMS, Vol. Eight**
Keith Laumer and others

G-16   **HORROR GEMS, Vol. Eight**
Algernon Blackwood and others

IN THE DAYS THAT FIRE WAS A GOD...

Try to imagine a world without fire. What would civilization be like? How would everyday life function without the benefit of a lighted match. Renowned science fiction author David H. Keller pondered those possibilities in his marvelous novel, "The Fireless Age." Keller laid out a bleak world where fire was a god—a god that no person was allowed to tamper with; and to do so was punishable by death. Keller's fireless world is a sometimes pleasant but more often than not, brutal realm. Set in pre-ice age North America, it's a world where dangers abound; from saber-tooth tigers to bloodthirsty, barbaric tribes. Keller's primary tribe, "The White Ones," harbors a long-standing initiation into manhood that is exceedingly bestial in nature, yet laden with a primitive sense of nobility. But Keller's main character, More Bear, is one of the few in his backward tribe to wonder what the benefits of fire would be for his world. In his quest for answers, More Bear sets out on a long journey filled with nail-biting primeval peril. From start to finish "The Fireless Age" is an exciting, sometimes thought-provoking prehistoric adventure.

ABOUT DAVID H. KELLER, M. D.

David H. Keller was born in Philadelphia in 1880. He was a significant writer of science fiction and fantasy during the golden age of pulp magazines.

Keller was also a psychiatrist, and is generally regarded as the first in his field to write science fiction literature. Keller graduated from medical school in 1903. After serving in the Army Medical Corps during WWI, he became the Assistant Superintendent of the State Mental Hospital in Prineville, Louisiana.

In 1928 Keller met with *Amazing Stories* editor Hugo Gernsback, who published Keller's first science fiction tale, "Revolt of the Pedestrians." Gernsback encouraged Keller to produce more works and the two established a long professional relationship that saw many of Keller's best works published not only in *Amazing Stories,* but also in Gernsback's later publications: *Wonder Stories, Air Wonder Stories,* and *Science Wonder Stories,* the latter of which showed Keller listed as Associate Science Editor.

The quality of Keller's writings was broadly entertaining, yet often intertwined with unusual themes and futuristic intuition, as well as controversial social ideas. He wrote dozens of short stories and numerous novel-length works, including "The Time Projector," "The Evening Star," "The Human Termites," "The Conquerors," and "The Metal Doom." Keller's tales were lovingly known by fans as "Keller yarns," a term coined by Hugo Gernsback himself.

After long and distinguished careers in both the literary and medical fields, David H. Keller passed away on July 13th, 1966.

THE FIRELESS
AGE

By
DAVID H. KELLER, M. D.

ARMCHAIR FICTION
PO Box 4369, Medford, Oregon 97504

FOREWARD

THE question may well be asked as to just what kind of civilization could develop without the use of fire?

Certainly, many parts of modern civilization would evolve without fire; people could learn to read, write, and even become cultured. In the future a similar question will be asked concerning the state of civilization had not the airplane, radio, and automobile been invented.

It is the author's opinion that a race would advance rather far without fire, probably not so comfortably or so rapidly. In this tale he has imagined such a race, a nation who knew fire, but for religious reasons, refused to use it and who even punished by death all who dared think of doing so.

This imagined race lived on the continent that centuries after was called North America. They settled the region from the Pocono Mountains, southward to the Gulf of Mexico, and westward to the Mississippi River. There they built cities, and rose to a high state of barbaric culture. They successfully fought lower races of mankind, who turned down into South America. The glacial period finally destroyed them and their cities, and only a few remained to sail eastward, probably to land on the island of Atlantis.

The story could be written in a dozen different ways by a dozen Science Fiction authors. It has numerous possibilities of variation. But always it has to show the determination of the developing man to use all natural resources in spite of superstition, custom, and the teaching of his religious leaders. It was a fireless age, but when necessity drove, it became an age of fire, used as a servant and not as one of the Half Gods of prehistoric ages.

CHAPTER ONE
The Boy Scouts Meet

THE Boy Scouts of Sylvania were gathering on Mount Minsi. Through the dense forests of white pine, spruce, and oak they had worked their way to the top of the mountain to hold their spring meeting.

Only the older boys were permitted to attend. The junior members of the association never made this hike till they were at least thirteen years old. The group, finally gathered on the top of the stone mass, overlooking the river, was remarkably uniform in size and appearance, as well as in age. A few older men were with them, not only as Scout Masters, but also as Care Takers. Any trip out of the cities into the dark forest was filled with danger. Every year there were fatalities, but the meeting had to be held. It was a part of the ceremonials, leading to manhood, to full membership in the White Ones.

From the rock covered top, they could see the river far below them. Many of the boys tried to throw stones into the water, but none was able to. Their school books told of a Scout Master, generations before, who could twirl a battle ax around his head and hurl it into the river from this ledge, but since his time, no one had been able to repeat his performance.

On the way up the mountain, there had been the usual chatter of happy, carefree boys. Once the groups met, the conversation died to whisperings. The four Scout Masters drew apart to exchange greetings, and to tell each other the news of their respective cities. Plans had to be perfected for the yearly inspection.

Four Scout Masters and one hundred Scouts were present. Twenty-five came from each city. Rarely any more, and never any less, except in the year of the Black Death, when the White Ones were so decimated that only thirty boys lived to make the trip.

"A fine lot of boys this year," commented Morrison, who came from the east of the river. "I have been a Scout Master for six years, and I have never seen a finer group. Our boys did well this year, studied hard, showed some initiative, and are in perfect health."

"Any losses?" asked Possert. "Our boys did well, but we had to send one into the long sleep. He talked too much. I think we have a little more trouble that way in the mountains than you do on the plains. After all, discipline must be preserved. We are so few in number that it will not do to have too much individuality at the expense of the community life."

"That is very true," replied Morrison. "We had nothing like that this year, but our traditions show that some time ago it was a serious matter. How is it on the other side of the Wind Gap, Hubler? Do you think there is any great difficulty in keeping the boys up to the mark? Are they following the traditions and the teachings of the Old Ones?"

"You bet they are. We have a system there. We keep them busy. That is the way to do with boys; keep them busy. Every program is so arranged that the boys have no leisure for insubordinate thinking. It does not make any difference if they are studying, working, or playing, every minute of their lives is supervised. It takes time and thought, but it pays in the long run. Of course, we have the slate-quarries there, and have to send roofing to all of the cities, and after a boy has worked with slate, he usually is too tired to do much thinking that is off the trail."

"Work is the solution, but it has to be filled with fun or it is hard business for youngsters," asserted Lawler, Scout Master from the plains south of the mountain. "We do a lot of farming down where we live, and I think our boys are happier working in the fields than yours are working in the slate-quarries or dark woods. But perhaps it is all in the way boys are brought up. Yet, in the way we do things, our boys are not as broad in their lives as I should like to see them. We raise farmers. Hubler's lads will all be slate workers. Possert's boys are woodsmen while Morrison's group would be lost in the woods, but they know a lot about clay working. I have thought for some time that the plan could be improved on. Have a rotating life for the four years before the last ceremonial. Have each boy spend one year north, east, west, and south of the mountain. Give them all the same education, but as far as their hands are concerned, broaden their abilities. Get the point? If you other Scout Masters think well of it, I am going to bring it to the attention of the Old Ones this year."

"It might work well, but I do not see any special use in it," replied Morrison. "I personally think that it is better for a boy to learn to do one thing well than four things poorly."

"I thought you would say that, but suppose something happens?"

"What do you mean?"

"Just this," insisted Lawler. "Suppose something like the Black Plague started over again? Let us imagine that it would be very bad in Hubler's sector. All the old persons die, all the teachers, most of the Scouts. Where would we get our slate from? You people east of the river know clay, but when it comes to slate, you are worthless. Not one of you has ever worked with slate. You would have to start at the beginning and learn, and it would take time; but if every man east of the river had spent a year of his Scout life working in the quarries, it would be simple to keep on with that part of the work of the White People. That is my point. We need a constant production of grain, wood, meat, slate, clay; and in order to get all these things, everyone should know a little about every kind of work."

"I thought the Old Ones decided five years ago that specialization was best," argued Morrison. "Find out what the boy wants to do, and then let him do it. I have a boy who loves chickens, and since he was ten we have been encouraging him in every way. Now, at fourteen, he knows a lot about it, and he has the finest flock I have ever seen."

"Same with our boys," agreed Possert. "One of our Scouts hunts bear. That is all he wants to do. Of course, he studies and works with wood, but every spare moment he has he is out after bears and he kills more than any other four of our Scouts."

"That is all true," sighed Lawler. "I know what the Old Ones decided, and I know what we have been doing, but sometime something is going to happen to us, and the White Ones will be fighting for their existence. The more things every member of the race knows how to do, the greater the chance of our surviving. Suppose we stop talking and start with the inspection? Boys are ready, I suppose?"

CHAPTER TWO
The Path to Manhood

THE boys were lined up in four rows. Slowly, the four Scout Masters inspected every boy; his teeth, muscles, clothing, his equipment for camping and his stone weapons. The clothing was a simple woolen shirt and drawers, with a skin fastened around the neck and covering the back. Shoes of cowhide were standard equipment, but the boys showed much individuality in their skins. Those from the mountains wore bear, lion, and deer skins; while cow, horse, and rabbit skins were used by the Scouts from the lowlands. The boys took a great deal of pride in this part of their clothing, which was more decorative than useful. Each lad carried a stone-tipped spear in his left hand, a stone hunting ax in his right hand and over his back was slung a quiver, filled with arrows and a bow. Since early childhood they had been well trained in the use of all these weapons. Some sectors of the White Ones had experimented with the sling, but it had never been standard equipment of the Scouts.

Every boy passed a perfect test, as far as physique, clothing, and arms went. The Scout Masters were pleased with the new group.

Possert, senior of the Scout Masters, then took charge of the meeting.

"None of you boys," he said from his position on the Speaker's Rock, "have ever been at this kind of Scout Meeting, but I know you all understand its purpose. Generations past, the White Ones had to fight for their existence. Sometimes they killed and sometimes they *were* killed. Since the Dark Ones died out, we no longer have to face human enemies, and even the animals we used to dread are no longer numerous enough to cause much trouble. But we must never forget the past. Say that with me."

The hundred Scouts and the three masters joined him in a deep chorus:

"WE MUST NEVER FORGET THE PAST!"

"And, because of this, we meet here today. This fall those of you who are worthy will be taken to our Sacred Place and given the final testing, which will end in your full citizenship. But first you must live through this day. In a cave near here we have placed a saber-tooth tiger. You will surround the cave, and when we open the door and he comes out, you are to kill him. Once he is killed, he is to be cut apart and eaten. Each of you must take a piece of his skin. Each of you must rub yourself with his blood. Each of you must take one of his bones, clean and polish it and keep it with you always. You have not fed for two sundowns, but now you can eat your kill. Thus, you will start to become real men. Thus it was in the old days. Repeat after me:"

"THUS IT WAS IN THE OLD DAYS!"

"And this is the path to manhood." The boys repeated after their leader.

"AND THIS IS THE PATH TO MANHOOD!"

In spite of all their lessons, few of them really realized what manhood meant to them. Certain things had to be done when they were six years old, other lessons had to be learned at eight and ten, and from ten on, life had been hard, constantly filled with toil, hardship, a steady bending of their independent spirits to the point at which they became a little part of a tribe instead of a large bit of individuality.

None of them had ever seen the beast that they soon would be called upon to kill. They knew about bears, mountain lions, and wild boars; but here was a thing, twelve feet long, shoulder high to their big men, an animal that had fangs twelve inches long, which could kill the largest bull with one paw stroke and carry it off on its back. The boys had to face it, fight it, kill it—and they were just boys. If this was life, it was hard life; it was a life different from any phase that they had ever seen. To become men, they had to go back to the perils of past ages; they had to forget their books, their chickens, their beautiful homes, their well kept farms.

Bodies, always kept clean, had to be covered with blood and offal, stomachs accustomed to decent food had to be filled with tiger meat. Always guarded carefully, the prize riches of their people, they were now on their own, to fight the most dangerous of the animals of the world.

This was their path to manhood. It was a pathway that their Scout Masters could show them, but on which they could not go on with them. No matter what happened, no matter how the battle waged, irrespective of how many boys were killed, they had to go on this pathway alone.

It was the path to manhood!

Ages before, the saber-tooth tigers almost outnumbered the White Ones. There was a time when no one could tell who would win the struggle, the animal or the man. Due to that struggle, man advanced in intelligence. The battle was finally decided by brains and not by brawn. The lesson was never forgotten; the Old Ones felt that it was vital that the young should have a terrible, real lesson, showing what had happened in the past. Tigers were caught each year in traps, tied and carried on carts till the caves were reached; and there liberated to teach the lesson of the past to the men of the future. In three other parts of the land three hundred other boys were waiting for the titanic struggle.

Four hundred boys! Never any more, and only rarely any less; the pick of all born fourteen years before, the survivors, the four hundred deemed worthy of life and manhood. Nice boys, well educated, in the best of health, were for one day thrown into the worst of past ages, to be prepared for the better things to come in future years.

Was it necessary? The Old Ones thought so.

Did the boys think so?

They did not think very much about the rightness, the ethics, the morality of the event they would soon be actors in.

All they thought of was that it was one of the things that they had to do to become men.

And they wanted to become men.

Each year they had seen some of their playmates disappear; boys who for this reason or another, could not pass the tests, could not measure up to the requirements, failed to show their ability to be worthwhile members of their sector. Now, in four sectors only one hundred were left. In the entire nation only four hundred lived to face the four tigers.

It was the path to manhood. For centuries not one of their male ancestors had failed to walk down that path. They knew that they would not fail.

They might die, but they would not fail!

CHAPTER THREE
The Tiger Kill

SLOWLY, they walked to a cleared spot on the mountain top, and formed a semicircle with the center a large black hole in a lofty rock. The hole was closed by a skillfully balanced rock. Behind the rock was the tiger without food for four days. The Scout Masters on the top of the cliff could liberate the tiger by pulling on a rope, tied to the stone. Once out, the only way of escape for the beast was through the ranks of the Boy Scouts. It could not climb the bare cliff, but it could crush through, break down, toss here and there the pieces of the living wall surrounding the mouth of the cave.

No doubt the tiger did not understand the part it was to play in the initiatory ceremonies; but it did know that it was a captive, anxious for freedom, a hungry animal, wanting food, a wild thing, determined to kill his worst and weakest enemy, mankind. Though there had been no preparatory practices, in spite of the fact that it had never faced Boy Scouts, there was no doubt about the fact that it would play his part well in the drama of life and death. For the boys it was the pathway to manhood, but to the tiger, it was a pathway to freedom.

The boys had been drilled in the part they were to play. Each was to shoot one arrow and then charge with his spear. After that the battle ax remained, his last resort.

The Masters from their vantage point on top the cliff waited till they were sure everything was ready. Then one dropped a white lamb skin down to the ground in front of the mouth of the cave. It was the signal. At once the four men started to pull on the rope, which threw the large stone out of plumb, off its center of gravity, and allowed it to roll to one side. Then they crouched on the rock and waited.

The boys, each with his bow-string stretched, arrow in place, ready to shoot, waited.

For a while the tiger waited, and then, it sprang.

In the air the arrows met it.

Landing on the ground, it sprang again, and this time met a wall of stone spear-points, but it reached the wall. With twelve inch fangs, with four terrific feet, armed with the sharpest of claws, it fought against the little beings who were trying to beat the last of life out of it with their battle axes. Filled with arrows, pierced through and through with spears, cut and pounded with stone axes, it fought on for two minutes, for five, and then came the end.

The tiger was dead.

And so were eight of the boys. Three were dying. Almost every boy had some injury. The Masters came down, and selected forty-four of the least seriously injured boys. Possert gave the order to them.

"Pick up these eleven Scouts and carry them to the edge of the mountain. Everybody come with us."

They picked up the eight dead and the three unconscious Scouts, and carried them on their shoulders. The other boys limped along as best they could. At the edge of the mountain they waited. Hundreds of feet below the river flowed, a glistening ribbon in the spring sunshine between the two walls of rock, clad with evergreens.

"Throw them over!" sharply commanded the Master. "At once!" he commanded, but with a break in his throat. Some of those boys he had taught for four years; one was his brother.

Through the air the eleven bodies hurled.

"And now, back to the tiger."

They limped back to the battle field and sat in a circle around their fallen enemy.

"Eat it!" Possert commanded. "Get your piece of skin. Get your cleaned bone. No one leaves here till all is eaten. Repeat after me, 'This is the path to manhood.' "

The eighty-nine Scouts and the three Masters joined him as they cried:

"THIS IS THE PATH TO MANHOOD!"

Bleeding, aching, suffering, they cut the beast up and ate the pieces. They scraped the bones and the hide. They licked the ground, covered with his blood clots. The four Masters watched them. At last Possert said, "It is enough. Form companies and be ready to march."

The sun was setting when they reached the river where they were allowed to bathe. The Masters gave the wounded first aid. Discipline was relaxed.

"You may sleep now till morning," explained Possert, kindly. "You have all done well. The kill of eleven is a record. Your names will be remembered by the White Ones. Sleep now. Tomorrow we will go back, each to his own sector, his own home."

In the soft glow of the twilight, each scout spread a bed of leaves, lay on it and covered himself as best he could with his back skin. In spite of their wounds and bruises and their unusual meal of tiger, they were soon fast asleep. The Scout Masters sat on the side of the river and watched the moon. There was little talking. Whatever each man thought, he kept to himself. Possert kept looking down the river, down to the sharp edge of the mountain, where he knew his dead brother lay among the hemlocks. The other three finally went to sleep. Possert was still awake when the sun rose.

Without breakfast, the Scouts, after a swim in the river, started back to their homes. It was regulations to eat nothing but tiger on this hike. They started silently with none of the usual chatter. A few days before they had been boys; now they were on the road to manhood.

CHAPTER FOUR
More Bear Goes Home

THE city of the northern sector had been built in a somewhat sheltered valley, but still near to the crest of the mountains north of the Water Gap. As far as architecture was concerned, it looked like the other cities of the White Ones. It was more of a house than a city, more of a beehive than a house. Built out of rocks, mortared together with mud, it was only two stories high, the first floor being dug into the rock and used only to keep cattle and supplies. At regular intervals in the roof of this first story, holes permitted the heat from the animal and the manure to partly warm at least the floor occupied by the families who had no other source of heat in the winter time. The windows were small and open except in the most severe weather, when they were covered with fine sheep skin, well greased, through which a little light came. The walls were hung with bear skins; the floors were covered with hay.

The White People lived without fire.

Never having used it, they did not need it. Their bodies never having been pampered, were cold resistant; their stomachs, never having had cooked food, were able to eat uncooked food. In fact, these White People of the northern sector rather prided themselves on the truth that they were stronger, larger, and healthier than some of the White Ones who lived in a warmer climate.

It was spring time. That meant house cleaning time in the community house. The hay used during the winter had to be taken out and the floors cleaned. The stables had to be emptied and the cattle taken to their pasture. The furs had to be aired and the windows opened. After a winter in the mountains it was good to be out in the sun again, without having to put furs on.

The boys of the Scout Troop came back home. Their reception was without outward emotion. Possert had taken twenty-five boys to the Water Gap. He brought back nineteen. His boys were hunters, fearless and accustomed to big game hunting. At the Tiger Kill they had led the attack without thought of self. Of the eleven who fell at the battle field, six had come from the north sector.

If the parents of the dead boys suffered, they did not show it. Pride of race, strength of personality, custom, developed through long years of cultural restraint, made it necessary for them not even to notice that their boys had not come home. Possert visited the Old Man of the sector and gave a short report, and life went on as usual.

One of the boys, More Bear, son of Many Bear, was an only son. His left thigh had been badly torn in the fight, and it had only been by the greatest effort that he had walked home. His mother washed the long cut, plastered it with healing herbs and made him comfortable on the best skins. Early in the afternoon the father joined them.

"Have a good trip, my son?" he asked.

"Fine."

"That is as it should be. For some years I have been making a medicine bag for you out of a beaver skin. I give it to you. In it I have placed the tooth of the sea cow that the man of our family brought many generations ago from the Great Sea. It is yours. Put your Tiger bone and Tiger fur in the bag with the tooth. Those of our family have always hunted, and you may become the greatest hunter of them all. But first you must become a man."

"I have started on the path."

"Tell me of the fight."

The mother silently came nearer, her eyes shining with pride.

"There were one hundred boys there. As we said when I first went to school, ten times the fingers on the two hands. Twenty-five boys from each sector. The clay boys, the slate boys and the farm boys were all there. A fine lot of fellows, but I think that our boys were a little larger. Every boy made perfect in regard to his equipment. Then the Masters let the tiger out. Of course, you had told me about the tigers, but Father, you should have seen this one. He was big, about twice as long as my spear, not counting his tail. I aimed my arrow at his eye as you advised me to, and then I went down on one knee, braced the end of my lance against the ground, and it went right into him as he sprang against it, and when he fell it broke in two. That was the end of the fight, as far as I was concerned. The beast fell on top of me and knocked my breath out of me, and when I was able to breathe again, he was dead. But I never let go of my battle ax."

"So you did not help to kill him?" asked the Mother.

"Let the boy tell the story in his own way, Lambkin," scolded the father, gently. "What happened then?"

"I did what I knew you would want me to. I hunted for my arrow and for my spear head. My arrow had gone through the eye into the brain. My spear head had pierced his heart. I knew this, but I did not boast of it. This is forbidden by the Scout Code. But I want to tell you and Mother about it, because, from my bear hunting, I know that I might have killed the Tiger single handed. I am but a boy, but some day when I am full grown I will go and try it. Have you ever heard of one of our hunters doing that, Father?"

The woman, Lambkin, smiled.

The man opened his medicine bag and took out two long polished teeth.

"A man once did that, and here are the fangs to show that he did. I am glad you are home, my son. Someday, when you are filled out and have your full height, I will go with you to the land of the Tigers and I will watch you make your solitary kill. But for a few years you had better practice on bears and mountain lions. Better get some sleep now. Tomorrow you must go back to school."

"The boys all did well," said More Bear. "Even the clay boys are fine Scouts."

"That is good. We need brave men to keep the White Ones alive," commented the mother.

CHAPTER FIVE
The Old Man

THE old man sat on the top of his home. The sunshine felt good to him. He was glad that he had lived through the winter to see another spring. It was always a pleasure to him to see the new green on the evergreens. In his heart there was a great love of the woods and the animals living in it.

Possert, the Scout Master, sat near him, telling him about the trip to the Water Gap and the ways of the boys in passing their test. Possert talked slowly, carefully, and in the greatest detail told of all that had happened from the time he and the Scouts had left the northern city till they had returned. In all of the report he entered into no personalities. He neither praised nor blamed any of the boys. They had lived up to the required standards of bravery. The sector had reason to be proud of them.

Cellar, the Old Man, smiled grimly as he heard of the fight.

"It is all good," he said. "So long as we have boys like that, the White Ones will live on. It is more important that we have brave men than that we have many men. And now let us forget for a while that I am a leader and you are a Master, and tell me about my Grandson, More Bear. How did he do?"

"About as you would expect. He shot his arrow, plunged his spear, and went asleep under the Tiger. When we came back, I watched him. The first thing he did was to hunt for his arrow and broken spear head. Some of the other boys did not care what they had done, but that lad wanted to see how close to the mark he had come. His arrow had gone into the eye socket and lodged in the brain. His spear head was in the Tiger's heart. I saw it all, but said nothing. He said nothing, but I bet he told his parents about it. No more than natural that he should. He is a great boy."

Cellar smiled. "I suppose the wise men in our race would say that it was hereditary. Those of our family have always hunted. Someday I will show you the book. A page for each generation, and on that page is painted the great kill by each great hunter of our family. Life at present is quiet. We even have to catch the tigers to use in the initiation ceremonies. But when we first came to this country, we were fortunate if the tigers did not get us first. I think about it a good deal.

Life is tame. New words are being used. At the last meeting of the Old Ones the students talked of things like higher education and culture and art. I listened and kept silent, but I had my own ideas. How about the other three centers? Will they send us our yearly supply of clay pots, slate and grain? Is there anything new? Is all well with them?"

"All seems to be as usual. Crops were good south of the mountain. We can have all the slate we need. The clay workers have a new method of making pots that will make them stronger and last longer. They asked if we wanted them painted. I said no, and that all we wanted was to have them strong and large enough to hold our food."

Just then a girl came up on the roof.

"One of our pigeons has just come from the west," she said. "It bore this message," She handed the Old One a small paper. He handed it to Possert.

"You read it," he commanded. "My eyesight is poor."

Possert opened it and read it silently.

"It is simply the annual message from the Center, telling that the Harvest meeting will be held as usual."

The Old Man turned to the girl. "

Send one of their pigeons back with this message," he ordered:

"THE HUNTING SECTOR OF SYLVANIA WILL BE REPRESENTED BY CELLAR, THE OLD MAN; POSSERT, THE SCOUT MASTER, NINETEEN INITIATES, AND FOUR WARRIORS."

The girl disappeared.

"What do you think of having the women take care of the carrier pigeons, Possert?" asked the Old Man.

"It seems to work out all right. At last I am in favor of it. In the future I believe we shall have to depend more on our women."

"Perhaps, but there is another side to it. In former times the women worked only in the home, and they had children. I married a well-educated woman, who in addition to her regular knowledge, wanted to study art. She became the pictorial historian of our four sectors. She even helped decorate the temple at the Center. But we only had one child, Many Bear. He wanted to marry Lambkin, who was a fine girl and made a fine wife, but she wanted to write. She had an idea that we should have books; so she took her skins and her pigments, and while her mother-in-law painted history, she wrote it, and they only had one child, More Bear. I know women, and so do you, who just stay at home and sew and cook, and they have lots of children. But they are few. It is all well enough to say that one brave man is better than many ordinary men, but when the White Ones came to this country, we had many men, and if we had not had many men, we should have been wiped out as the sun wipes out the frost on a fall morning. We are a great people, but we shall die as the elephant died in this country, unless we have more children."

Possert was silent. His wife spent hours breeding glowworms and fireflies. She felt that someday they could be grown big enough and kept alive long enough to be of real use for lighting the inside of their homes during the dark hours. Because she had insisted, he had taken her for a long trip to the south, to learn how the White Ones there used glowworms for illumination. Possert was proud of his wife, but they only had one child, and that one was a girl, who was working in the pigeon houses.

After a long silence, Cellar gave his orders, "Go on working with the boys. Teach them all you know. If you need help in any direction, ask for it. In one month we will start on the journey, I will select the warriors; if my memory does not fail me, there are still some men who have not made the journey since they were boys. Be ready in a month. All is well, except for the women. If they keep on being more interested in all these other forms of work and less interested in their homes and families, the time will come when there will be an end to the White Ones."

"Shall you march the whole distance? Or shall you try something new and use some of the sail roads?"

"I think that we had better walk. A few horses to carry the packs, but we will walk. But tell me again about that road you saw last year."

"It looked like a good idea to me. One of the shore sectors started it on the beach. The idea was that if wind could make a boat go on the water, wind could make a cart go on the land. It worked well on the hard beach, but the hard beach was only by the water. So they made long narrow beaches out of tree trunks, laid end to end, with long slots in them to hold the wheels. I saw such a beach on the prairie. It was as long as a man could walk in a day, but the cart went from one end to another in a little time when the wind blew hard. I could run faster than the cart went, but when I walked, it passed me."

"And our men sat in the cart?"

"Yes, and carried their hay in it. But when the wind blew day after day in one direction, they had to use horses to take it back to the other end."

"I can walk to a place and back again, no matter how the wind blows, and my horse can also," replied the Old Man scornfully. "Why should I use something that can only go one way and then has to have horses take it back? No, it may do for the weak ones who have little legs, but I will go on as my Fathers went on."

Possert started to frown.

"There is another thing about it that will force them to stop it. I heard whispers of it. When the wind blows strong and the cart goes fast, the hubs of the wheels become hot, as the result of a summer sun on a rock. Once a man saw a fog come from the wheels."

"What do you mean?"

"Just that. It looks as though the God did not approve of it. The men running the sail cart would not speak of these things to me, but I was told they had to stop the cart often and put more fat on the hubs. But I know and you know what the end will be, if the Old Men in the center realize the danger. It will be death to the men of the shore who are playing with forbidden things."

"Did you by any chance ride in this sail cart?"

"I did not, but I wanted to. At the same time I would never dare to get in one when the wind was blowing strong."

"I will walk!" cried the Old Man.

CHAPTER SIX
Children in Love

MORE BEAR kept quiet for three days and at the end of that time his leg was nearly healed. He was anxious to leave the house. There was something he was anxious to do, someone he wanted to see very badly. He dressed in a new scout uniform that his mother had made for him, hung a very special bear skin over his shoulder, and with his bow and quiver on his back and his spear and battle ax in his hands, he very casually, and very proudly left his home and walked away slowly from the little city. Little children called him by name; girls and women shouted that they were glad to see him out again; even the men he passed welcomed him. He felt that he was certainly growing up.

Out in the dark forest he met White Pigeon, Possert's daughter, the girl who was starting to work with the carrier pigeons, the one who had brought the message to the Old Man. She was only thirteen years old, but she already knew more about pigeons, how to breed them for speed and homing qualities, how to handle them, and write and send messages, than anyone else in the sector. She was a lovely child, blond, with long yellow hair, and though More Bear was a year older, she was a little taller, as she had almost reached her full height, while he would keep on growing for at least two more years.

They had known each other since early childhood, played together, gone to school together. They had even gone hunting with each other. The older people took it for granted that some day they would marry.

"You are almost a man now," she said when she met him.

"Almost," he said, kissing her. "At least I have started on the path. We had a great hike this time, but I did miss you. Guess we have to get used to these separations. But when I am full man and we are married we can be together a lot. In fact, I have been wondering how you would like to live apart for a few years? It has been done, you know, and all we have to do is to get permission from the Old Man. I know a dandy cave, and I am sure we could get along all right."

The girl frowned.

"You mean be away from the city for two or three years?"

"That is just what I mean. We will go bear hunting, and fishing and pick nuts and berries and swim and all that sort of thing."

"That would be fine. I should like it a lot, only I do not see how I could do it."

"Why not?"

"What would my pigeons do without me?"

"Do you love those silly birds more than you do me?"

"You know I don't, but that is my work, just as bear hunting is your work. If we marry and live in the city, I could take care of our home and look after the pigeons at the same time, but I do not see how I could possibly carry on if I lived with you in a cave. Not that I do not want to do it, I should rather live with you in a cave than with any other man in the best home in our city, but I just have to take care of the pigeons. In a few years I shall be in complete charge. This morning I carried and sent messages for the Old Man. Think of that!"

The boy smiled sadly.

"I guess you women are all alike. I talked to Father about it last night, and he said he wanted to live in a cave when they first married, but Mother wanted to be where she could go on making books. Suppose we go down to the lake and go swimming? We both enjoy that, and probably the cold water will put some common sense into your brain."

In the ice cold water More Bear showed that he was the stronger, but White Pigeon was able to beat him to the other shore. She had a stroke that few of the men were able to learn. Making use of this, she reached the shore, waded out of the water and was starting to wring the water out of her hair while the boy was still twenty feet from shore.

Suddenly, he called, "Jump!"

Surprised, she looked at his frightened face and then turned around to see what had caused his alarm. There, in the bushes, crouched ready to spring at her, was a mountain lion. She started to run for the edge of the lake, stumbled on a stone and fell forward just as the lion sprang.

More Bear, still in the water, realized but too late that he had done something no Scout should have done. He had left every weapon on the other side of the lake. He did not have even his short, stone hunting knife. And there was his girl, his woman, his future mate on the ground, and the lion would reach her in a few seconds. Stumbling through the shallow water, he picked up a large cobblestone and threw it. It struck the lion on the nose, not the most dangerous spot, but certainly the most sensitive one. For a second it diverted the beast's attention from the prostrate girl to the boy. The lion paused, snarling, undecided as to the action of the next second. That moment's hesitation was fatal. Another stone, larger, sharper, struck it, this time between the eyes, and another and still another found the mark. The girl, springing to her feet, ran to the water and threw herself in, and started to swim to safety.

The boy joined her, and a few feet away from the shore they turned to look at the mountain lion, which stayed at the edge of the lake. Then, slowly, the young couple, side by side this time, the race over, the thought of disaster still with them, swam back to their clothing and safety. White Pigeon put on her clothing, but More Bear simply hung his hunting knife around his neck and took his spear in his hand.

"What are you going to do?" asked the girl.

"I am going back to kill that lion," he replied as he started to swim back across the lake. "No lion can treat you that way, and keep on living."

She picked up his quiver with the bow and arrows and started to run around the shore of the lake. He was skinning the dead beast by the time she reached him.

"It will make a fine skin for the cave," he explained. "Full grown lion and in fine condition. But we must be careful. We think that just because nothing ever happens, nothing ever will happen, and then when we least expect it, something does happen. I never realized how much I loved you till I thought I had lost you. I want you to promise to marry me just as soon as I am admitted to full manhood by the Old Ones of the nation."

"I have always wanted to be your woman," replied the girl, and she laughed a little, even though tears were in her eyes. "And, if you want me to go and live in a cave, I will do even that."

So they arranged matters as they walked back to their city, carrying between them the lion skin. But More Bear had a peculiar feeling that, when the time came, they would live in the city and she would keep on taking care of the pigeons, just as his mother kept on making books and his grandmother kept on painting pictures.

CHAPTER SEVEN
Temple of the Fire God

IN practically the geographical center of the nation the White Ones had built a meeting place. It was not a city, for few lived there the year around; it was not a trade center, for it was far off the beaten pathways of the race; it was intended for one thing and one thing only.

Surrounded by lofty mountains, hidden on all sides by mountain crags, covered with virgin timber, visible only to the eye of the soaring eagle, the small cup-shaped valley lay, less than a half mile in diameter. In its exact center was a building, empty, except for a large circular stone. The stone was concave, and in it had burned for many centuries the Fire, Sacred God of the White Ones.

It was a fireless age, but it was not without knowledge of fire.

Fire was the God, and not the servant of the race.

Children were born, grew to become adults, died as seniles; springs were followed by summers and winters; years came and died; but the God never died!

Hour after hour, day after day, year by year four chosen men watched it, fed it, cleaned it, so that it would live on.

Two by night and two by day for one year, and then four more men for another year.

This was the Center of the race, the altar of the God, the place every male had to visit at least once in his life before he could become a man. In this building decisions were made, the future was provided for, trials were held here, and punishments given. The God consumed not only wood, but members of the race found guilty of law violation.

By the fire, on a chair of gold, the Old Old Man of the White Ones rested throughout the year, waiting.

The chair of gold had been built through the centuries, gradually growing larger as it had been added to. Pounded into shape by stone hammers, like the Fire God, it was a symbol. The Fire was God in a spiritual sense. The Old Old Man was God in a material sense. He lived in the Temple till he died, and was replaced by the oldest of the Old Men of the race. The four chosen men cared for both gods, loving the one and fearing the other.

The time for the Harvest Celebration had come. From four directions the worshippers were arriving at the Temple. At last they were all there—The Fire God on the altar—The Old Old Man on his gold chair—sixteen Old Men seated on the stone floor around him.

Sixteen Scout Masters and a few over three hundred Initiates, the chosen Boy Scouts, who had faced the Tigers and were now ready to be made men were there. They stood in orderly fashion, silent, straight—wonderful examples of adolescent manhood.

The Old Old Man stood up and started addressing the boys.

"You have come here to take the last steps on the road to manhood. I know that so far all of you have been found worthy to become men. First, you must know about our God.

"Many years ago, many hundreds of years ago our race knew what fire was. It was used to heat the caves, to fight wild beasts, to cook the food with. To us, it was like water, wind, and rock. At that time we did not know it was a God and would become angry if it were treated as a servant. At a harvest festival all the race was gathered in the dark forest. All that year there had been no rain. The leaves were dry, the woods were dry. Each family had a fire. In the center of the camp there was a large fire. One night the terrible God sent wind, a, great wind without rain. By the wind he scattered parts of himself through the woods, and they burned with a great burning. Our race fled before the angry One, but they could not run as fast as the God could fly though the air. He was determined to kill our race for our sins against his greatness. He followed us to the shore of the great ocean and not till we hid in it were we safe.

"Tradition says that less than one hundred reached the safe ocean. All the rest of a great race were sacrificed to the angry God. Rough rafts were built, and on them the great ocean was crossed. Only sixty-five lived to see the new land.

"Those men and women were brave, intelligent, industrious. From them our race has grown. We knew men, we knew nature, we knew the wild beasts. We conquered everything. We survived. We feared nothing but the God Fire. This temple was built, the altar carved and the Fire was placed on it and fed.

"It is a God, a Great God.

"Never again will we use it as a servant. Once we were taught the lesson. If Fire has to teach us again, we will be destroyed utterly. You will now raise your right hand and give the promise.

"We will never use Fire.

"We will not use Fire to warm our bodies, cook our food, work our metals, fight our battles.

"We will never use Fire. "The penalty is Death!"
"DEATH!"

Part by part he said it and part by part they repeated it after him.

The Old Old Man turned to the sixteen Old Men behind him.

"These Initiates have been judged worthy of manhood. Are all of you satisfied as to their ability to become men?"

"We are," was the reply.

"They must make the blood sacrifice to our God of Fire."

Old Man Cellar walked up to the altar. By right of age he ranked the others. He was older in years, but younger in general appearance. As he moved forward, Possert, the Scout Master, also walked to the center of the Temple, followed by his scouts. Possert took the first lad by the left wrist and extended it to the Old Man who took the little finger and swiftly amputated the last joint with a knife of obsidian. The little-finger end was thrown on the Fire God and the next candidate for manhood came forward. In a little time the mountain boys by their blood offering, had become mountain men.

Without delay, Old Man after Old Man sacrificed the Scouts from his sector. It was a token sacrifice, a part for the whole, a traditional memory of the time when the Fire God had demanded entire bodies, almost the entire nation, as a burnt offering to his offended majesty.

Finally, all the boys had become men. The Harvest had been completed, as far as that part of the ceremony was concerned. Once again the audience stood in rigid rows around the sides of the Temple.

Then the Old Old Man cried, "You are now men. You have finished the road!"

And the new adults of the White Ones cried after him: "We are Men!"

One of the Old Men came to the front of the altar.

"Judgment!" he cried. "One of my men has broken the Law. I ask that he be tried."

"What has he done?" asked the Old Old Man.

"He left my city and was gone for two years. When we found him, he was in a cave and had the Fire God with him. Let him tell the tale."

"Let him tell it," agreed the Ruler.

Two guards brought him in, not bound, but a captive.

"Tell your tale," was the command.

"It is worth telling," replied the man.

CHAPTER EIGHT
One Man Leaves the Path

"YOU all know that we have no metals we can work with. Gold, copper, and a little tin.

All are soft; they will not cut, they will not hold an edge. What is the result? We work with stone. Think of it? Stone, when our mountains are filled with iron. Trying to cut down trees and work the wood with stone, when we could have iron. I am a metal worker. All that the White Ones knew about metals I knew. But I wanted to know more. So I left my sector and lived by myself for two years. I used the Fire God. I tamed him on my forge. He never hurt me; he would not hurt anyone who was careful. I experimented with iron ore, burnt out the dross, made pieces of pure iron. I learned how to harden it, give it shape, an edge. I learned how to put pieces of sharp iron on the end of a stick so I could cut things with it. It was fun to cut down a tree with my tools. I made little pieces of iron to drive through two pieces of wood to hold them together. I made needles out of it to sew with, so the women would not have to use bone anymore. I made iron fingers to hold the hot metal and iron pounders to shape it.

"The Old Man found me. He said I had broken the law. I was just trying to make things easier for our people. Some day we shall be found by a nation who has iron weapons, and they will break us, as children break a bird's egg. I am offering you tools, weapons. There is no telling what use you can make of a hard metal that can be shaped and given a cutting edge. But to work this black stone that turns to metal, you must use Fire. Have I done wrong? Look at this knife. You can cut hair with it."

He handed the knife to the Old Old Man, who took it, felt its edge and then handed it to the other Old Men for their inspection. The ancient made no comments, but sat with his eyes closed. Suddenly he slumped downward in his chair.

He died as he lived, a Ruler of his people.

They took him out of the Temple.

Cellar walked up and sat down in the gold chair.

"You know the law," he cried. "I am the oldest of the Old Men, and now I am the Old Old Man. What do you say concerning this prisoner?"

"He has broken the Law!" The Old Men cried.

"What is the penalty?"

"Death!" was the low answer.

The man in the gold chair turned to the prisoner.

"I listened to everything you had to say. I am sure that much of what you said was true, but the safety of our nation must come first. It matters not if we have to fight with weapons of stone, work with tools of stone, eat our grain and meat as we find it, sleep in houses that are cold in winter. Nothing counts that happens to the individual, if only the nation can go on living. Once our God was offended because we used him for a servant. He killed all but a few, but those learned the lesson. You have broken the Law. More Bear! Come here…"

The young man, only a few hours ago a boy, came up to the gold chair.

"This man has wandered away from the path of manhood. Kill him!" the Ruler commanded.

More Bear hesitated, then swung his lance forward and thrust it through the prisoner's body, so far that the stone head came out the back.

"Give him to the God!" Cellar ordered, and the guards placed the body of the dead man on the flames.

The Scout Masters and the new men of the nation left the Temple. Only the Old Men remained.

"You can now report to me the condition of our people," the new Ruler said.

One at a time the Old Men read their reports, the number of children born during the year, the number of deaths, of marriages, the condition of the harvest, the success of the hunting, the new inventions to make life easier. Cellar heard them all without comment, up to the very last man.

Then he said, "I come from the dark forest. We love trees and hunting. I have watched trees grow. The oak lives a long time but it must keep on growing a little larger every year. When it ceases to grow, it begins to die. The White People have ceased to grow. We will die. We have too many deaths and too few births. What do our wise healers say?"

"We have had hard winters," answered one from the South. "Even in our warm lands the winters have been bitter. Our women are bitter. They say, 'Why should we bring children into the world if we cannot feed and keep them warm in winter?'"

"Are we growing tender?" asked Cellar.

"No, but our women are growing intelligent. We men know the Law, but the women have never been to the

Temple. They know our God only by tradition. They are talking."

"Talking of what?" asked the new Old Old Man, sharply.

"Of keeping their children warm and giving them better food, and whether it would be worthwhile to move the entire nation to the far South, where there is no winter. They argue about the sun, and even my wife says that the sun is the true God and that the Fire God we men worship is only a symbol of the sun."

"Why don't you make them stop talking?"

"Can you?"

"No. But we are men, and we have the Law, and we know the danger; so we will follow the path. Perhaps we have been giving the women too much education, too many advantages, too much freedom."

"We have not given them anything," countered another man. "What they have, they took without asking, and they take what they want. They are restless. Some women even want to come to the Temple. They say that they are equal with men. Our women even threaten to take the young children, go far south and leave us forever."

"That might have some advantages," said Cellar, smiling. "But if you men cannot hold your women, you are not entitled to have women. I will think over all this during the next year as I sit in the gold chair and watch the worship of the Fire God. You think over it in your sectors, and next year we will talk about it. Leave me and go. Teach the young men the Law. See that they follow the path. As for the women, we shall have to do what we can with them. I have lived with one many years. She is a fine woman, and I love her dearly, but I never have understood her."

After the meeting of the Old Men, Cellar sent for Possert.

"You shall have to tell the mountain people the news," he said gently. "Be sure my wife knows that this is none of my doing and not to my desires. I've always been active, and to sit in a gold chair till I die is something I shall have to learn to do. There's no need of telling my son to look after his mother, for he will do that without the telling. Say to all that it is my wish they do not depart from the path. I suppose Fastfoot will become the Old Man of our sector. I have known him since a boy. He is to be trusted. Have you anything to say?"

"One thing. Why did you have the boy do it? That was man's work."

"More Bear is my grandson. In many ways he is a different boy from the others. I have talked to him, and he is a thinker. There was a fear in my heart that he would someday think too much and depart from the path. I watched him as the prisoner told his story, and in my grandson's eye was agleam as the tale of iron and sharp weapons was told us. I wanted to teach him that no one could wander from the path and live on, and my way of teaching him was to make him the executioner of the lawbreaker."

"He did as you commanded," the Scout Master replied. "He did it without answer or argument, but it hurt him. You gave him an injury today that he will never forget and maybe never forgive. You are the Old Old Man, and I know that I should not talk in this way to you, but you might have told one of the older men to do this thing and not a boy."

"I want him to be a man!"

"He is one! But I do not think you were wise."

CHAPTER NINE
More Bear Travels Alone

THE next morning most of the men left the Center and the Temple. The men from the mountain had been the first to leave. All that day they walked through the forest. At night they prepared to sleep.

More Bear asked the Master to come a little apart from the group.

"I want to talk to you," he said.

"What is it?"

"Am I now a man?"

"You are."

"I know I am. I have my tiger skin and tiger bone and my medicine bag. I have passed the tests and been sacrificed to the Fire God. I have taken the vows and been accepted by the council of Old Men. So I am a man. I have my rights. I, now, according to the Law, tell you that I am going on a lone journey, and according to the Law you cannot say 'no' to me."

Possert looked at the fifteen-year-old boy, now called a man. With some of his sector he would have argued, given advice, but not with this man. So he simply said, "That is your right. May you come back safe. Any messages?"

"Yes. Tell my parents what was done, and say to your daughter, White Pigeon, that when I come back, knowing more than I do now, we will go on with our plans. That is all. I leave you in the morning."

When the men awoke the following day, one man was missing. He had thought it best to leave before his fellow mountain men knew what he was doing. He did not want any company.

For the next two years More Bear wandered through the land of the White Ones. He visited every sector, and studied the little individual habits of each city.

He fished on the South Gulf with the sea folk, hunted buffalo with the men living west of the mountains. He rode in the sail cart and learned how to make it start and stop. Far South he lived with the White Ones, who dwelt in the houses without walls on account of the heat, and kept large fire beetles in cages to give them light at night. He even, to the great astonishment of the Professors, went to the college of the race, and asked to be told more of geography, and metals, and winds and weathers and all that there was new in writing and the making of books and the reading of them. He was the first man who had ever said:

"Don't tell me what you think I should know. Just answer my questions, for I am the only one who knows best what I want to learn."

At last he was ready to return to his city, and always peculiar and very individualistic, he decided to go in a bee-line rather than to follow the beaten roads. So with the peculiar homing instinct of a carrier pigeon, he started up and down mountains and over streams. He lived on the country, hunting game and picking grain and fruits as he went.

One day, far ahead of him, he saw something curling languidly up above the trees on the mountain ahead of him. That was new, something he did not know about, something that he had to investigate; so he walked carefully and finally crept up the mountain above the curling thing that he might look down on it. He saw it was coming out of a hole in the side of the rock, and below there was a little noise.

He knew about caves, and he was sure that there was a cave there, and that some thing or some one was in that cave; so he worked his way very gradually around to find the opening. There were signs of life there, and human life at that. To More Bear that meant only one thing, and that was that the cave was occupied by one of the White People. He knew there were other people in the world, but no one of his race had ever seen them, and there certainly were none around there.

He waited till night, and then he climbed a tree from which he could see the mouth of the cave. Morning brought him what he wanted to see. A man came out from the cave. More Bear did not see any reason now for either fear or caution; so he climbed down the tree and ran to the man, his right hand outstretched, palm forward to show that he had no knife in it, which was the peace greeting of the nation. To his surprise, the man threw his spear at him. The mountain man dodged, jumped forward, and with bare hands made him prisoner. It was not a fair contest, as the stranger was little and hardly more than a child in More Bear's hands.

"I came to you in peace!" demanded the victor. "Why did you try to kill me?"

"Because I was sure you would kill me!"

"Why should I kill you?"

"Because of the path. Because I have broken the Law. I thought they had found me and had sent you to kill me."

The mountain man released the little man.

"What Law have you broken?" he demanded.

"The Law of the Fire God. I use it as my servant."

"In the cave?"

"Yes. I have lived here for three years."

"So that is it. Show me your sin."

"Come and see. But you will not kill me?"

"I will not kill you."

"But what of the oath?"

"That is for the Old Old Man to say. I killed once, because he ordered me. The man I slew was young; he knew a great deal. It seemed to me that he was a good man, but I killed him because I was told to do so by the Old Old Man. But the Old Old Man is far away now, and I cannot hear his orders. You are safe."

"Then I will show you. Come with me into the cave."

There was only one door to the cave. It was fall. The leaves had turned purple and gold; there was a chill of winter approaching, but the cave was warm. In the center was a large, oval shaped rock, flat on top, and there were things on that rock that More Bear had never seen.

CHAPTER TEN
Fire Becomes a Servant

"I AM going to ask you some questions first," said the stranger. "Do you eat wheat and corn? If you do, how do you prepare it?"

"We grind it. Many years ago we used two rocks and ground it, a grain or two at a time. Then we mixed it with water or milk and made cakes of it, and we placed those cakes on the hot rocks, heated by the summer sun. When they became hard and dry, we put them away in reed baskets, and kept them against the day of our hunger in the winter time. Later on we learned to make two rocks rub against each other by means of water power. A dam was built, and the water, falling down, turned a wooden wheel. In places where the wind blows we learned to use the wind to turn the wheels. With these improvements, we could make more flour. Beyond the mountains are the grain growers. They have good harvests and always wind; so they make flour for other centers. That is how we use the corn and wheat. Did you know that?"

"I did. When I became a man I went on the lone journey, as you seem to be doing now. I saw everything and learned all that I could, but I was not content. I think that it was because I always had pain inside of me. It was hard for me to eat, especially in winter time. So I came here, and started to conquer the Fire God. First I found him in the woods where he had come down and hit a tree with his fire finger. But later I learned to make him.

"Yes. I found him in two pieces of wood that I rubbed together. He was little at first, like an unborn child, but I fed

him, and he grew. I can make him now anytime. I said
something then, and I will say it to you, even though you kill
me. *If I can make a God, then I am a greater God than he is!*

"I took the Fire God and made him work for me. When I
killed a bird or a rabbit, I put him near the God and ate, and
when I ate that food I did not have the pain inside of me. If
I made the fire large enough I was warm in winter. More and
more I learned about Him; then I started in to build these
things you see. I found that he had a breath, and I made a
place for Him to live in and breathe through. That was five
years ago. The work I did then I tore down. I was not
satisfied, but at last I learned the great secret. I found that
His breath could be put into water.

"Do you see that white vessel there? It is made of clay, a
very strong clay that was able to stay together, no matter how
angry the God became. Perhaps the learned word and metal
men have a name for it. I put the Fire under it and water in
the vessel, and from the water came the breath of the God,
and that breath looked like a white cloud. I made another
vessel with just a small opening in it, and then the breath
came out like wind. When I put a little windmill in front of it,
the wheels turned, just as the windmills that grind grain in the
west. After months of hard work I made a little mill and
found that, with the breath of the Fire God, I could turn the
stone mill and grind corn. I can show you if you will not kill
me. I grind just one grain of corn at a time, because it is all
very small, just like a humming bird.

"All the time I was looking for different food, food I
could eat and live on without the pain inside me. I found that
meat placed in the hot water was good; the water was good to
drink. And I took the corn cakes and placed them on top of
the God and that was good. So at last, with this new food,
prepared by making the Fire God work for me, I grew strong
and the pain left me."

"But you grind but one grain of corn at a time?" argued More Bear. "A child could do that with two stones."

"But suppose it was made larger, this thing I have made? Suppose it was very large? Then the corn and wheat could be ground a basket at a time. But to do that more than one man would have to know my secret. If it were large the grain could be ground at any time, even if the stream of water was frozen or dry and the wind did not blow. And if the women and little children ate the meat from the water and drank the water the meat was in, and if the men ate the meat and the cakes cooked in this new way, the whole of the *White People would grow stronger.*"

"We are strong enough!"

"Some are, but others are weak and have pains as I had."

"Show me. Make the wheels go around."

The stranger put more food, food of twigs and bark into the Fire God, and soon little wheels and pieces of stone started to move on the top of the flat stone, and between two revolving stones the stranger dropped a grain of corn. It slowly became powder.

"What do you call this breath of the Fire God?" asked More Bear.

"Good. I had to have a name for it. I talk to myself, since for years I have seen no one and I did not want to forget how to talk. To all these things that I made I gave names. This breath flowed like a stream of water. It was a stream, but not a stream. So I changed the sound to make me think of a stream and also because it had a sound like the hissing of a snake, *sssssssss*. I made the name steam. Say it after me, steam; get that *sssssssss* sound?"

The hunter said it. He listened to it. He said it again.

"This is a very evil thing you have done," at last he whispered, "but it is also a very wonderful thing. The man I killed made a servant of the Fire God and took metals and gave them a sharp edge. That was also evil, but it was wonderful. You work with food, and he worked with metals, and because he broke the Law, he is dead, and if the Old Old Man knew of your work, you also would die. Is there iron in these mountains? If there is, I will stay here with you and learn to make a sharp knife, and teach you, and you will teach me, for it is not good that this thing you have learned should be lost."

"Will you also break the Law?" asked the stranger in astonishment.

"I will. If this Fire is really a God, then I will die for my sin, but if He is just a servant, who should fear Him? I shall soon be seventeen years old, and I shall have much to do in life if I live to be an old man. Hurry and teach me. How do you feed the Fire? And what is your name? No, do not tell me. I will give you a new name. I am called More Bear because I am even now a mighty hunter, but you shall be called Fire-Man, because you have made of the God a servant of a man."

CHAPTER ELEVEN
Death of the Grain Growers

FROM the west; land of the Grain Growers, land of the setting sun and windmills, came pigeons, bearing sad news. The messages were brought to the Old Old Man as he sat stately and dignified on his golden chair. Each pigeon brought a few words. The entire story was told by putting these words together. It was read to the Old Old Man.

"We are being killed by a new race of men. Our fields are destroyed; our men torn to pieces; our windmills torn down. These men are big like lions, and as many as grasshoppers from the western mountains. Now, our Center is swarmed on, and soon we shall all die. The White People are few.

Warn all of them, or soon all the Centers will be as ours, the stones torn apart and our bones among the stones."

"Leave me," the Old Old Man commanded, "and come back tomorrow. I want to think over these things."

The next day he commanded that carrier pigeons be sent to all the Centers, ordering, the Old Men to come as rapidly as possible to him.

Then he waited. There was nothing else to do.

Compared with others in the race, he was not a highly educated man. He had a sufficient degree of native intelligence, but not very much learning derived from books or attendance at one of the small colleges of the country. Most of his life he had lived in the mountains, hunting. Now, as the Old Old Man (simply because he was the oldest of the Old Men), he felt the responsibility of making decisions affecting the very life of his nation. He decided to send for the college man who had the greatest reputation for the wisdom of books, and to talk with him while waiting for the Old Men to answer his command.

One of the Centers had gradually grown into a service station for information. Just as there were Centers for grain growing and clay working and animal industries, so there was a center for learning. Any young man or woman showing unusual mental ability could visit one of these houses in this special Center and stay as long as desirable. In fact, he could make it a permanent home if he showed teaching ability. There the books and instruments of the White People were collected.

Know-More was not the Old Man of that Center, but of all the learned men in the Educational Center, he was credited with being the man who had the greatest general knowledge. In three days, traveling in a litter, carried by young men, he came to the Temple where the Old Old Man awaited him. There was little ceremony in the greeting exchanged. The

Message carried by the pigeons was given to him. He had already heard the news.

"Who are the people who have destroyed our Grain Center?" demanded the Ruler. "Who are they and where do they come from?"

"I do not know."

"I thought you knew everything?"

"I do not. This is what I do know. Many years ago we fled from the anger of our Fire God. A few of us were able to cross the great water, and we came here. Long after we came here we learned to write marks on skins and gave to each mark a sound, and thus books were formed. In these first books were put what the Old Men remembered of the tales told them by other Old Men. One Old Man remembered more than the others, though, perhaps he dreamed dreams and thought them memories. They were stories of the past, his stories of the past; so when we wrote them on skins we called them first "His Stories" and later on simply "Histories." What I know of the past I learned by reading those books.

"When we came to this land there were no people here. Animals, birds, trees, but no people. And we have never found any signs that there had ever been any people here, no fallen walls of cities or burial places of the dead.

"Since we came across the great water, none of us have ever dared to go back. All, we know of land and water is what we have learned by living here. We know of the water towards the rising of the sun. We know there is a lot of water toward the hot lands. This side of the Grain Center there is a mighty river. We know there are mighty mountains on the other side, but no one has ever dared to cross them.

"For many years we have lived here. How long? It is hard to tell, but in our books are written the names of over two hundred Old Old Men who have sat here in this golden chair, even sat here before there was a gold chair. But never has there been word of other peoples.

"Our dreamers have talked about other races of men. Dreamers, not practical men. Perhaps you have never talked to one of them? They use peculiar language. They say again and again, 'I think,' which is simply their way of saying, 'I dream.' A very favorite idea of theirs is this, 'Because we live as a nation, there must be other nations somewhere. When they are asked to show that this is true, they only reply that they think so. They think that because there are different kinds of animals there must be different kinds of men.

"The thing that has happened shows that for once their dreams were true ones. This race of men has come from the lands of the setting sun. They must have crossed the mountains. They seem to be more like wild animals than like men, because they kill and destroy and tear down. Our grain growers were hunters, but only in a small way. They could not fight with the same skill that others of our Centers could have fought with, such as the mountain people that you came from. The Center in the lion country might have given a different answer in this fight. But perhaps not. The message says that these wild men were mighty in number, even as grasshoppers, and in the Grain Center there could not have been more than three hundred men, women and children. They have been destroyed—their Center torn down. And the grasshoppers move on. Big as lions, they move on. We capture the lions; every year we take sixteen of them to help our boys learn the pathway to manhood, but they have to be caught in pits, and bound with ropes. Suppose they were as many as grasshoppers? What could we do?"

"I have killed a lion by myself!" was the proud answer.

"I know; but could you keep on doing it all day? And all the next day? And the next? And the next? What if they came at you fifty at a time? Or a hundred in a day?"

"I understand," acknowledged the Old Old Man. "It would be the end of the race. But something must be done. In some way they must be stopped, or the White People die. In your Center you have all the wise men. This is my command. Go back to them and make plans. Use your wisdom. Learn how to kill faster. After all, these strangers are animals and we are men. Up to this time, no kind of animal has been great enough or strong enough or so many that we could not destroy them or tame them. These dreamers! They were able to think of other races of men. Tell them to go on thinking, keep on dreaming, and see if they cannot find a way to save our people. Go at once and get to work. And when the Old Men come to my call, I will send for you."

CHAPTER TWELVE
The Lion Hunter's Strike

OF ALL the sixteen Centers there was none more peculiar in its national work than the Lion Center. Their specialty was the capturing of the Saber Tooth Tigers or Lions needed every year for the initiatory services of the Boy Scouts. These animals bred in the warm woods east of the great river. At one time they had been so many that they threatened the very life of the White Ones. Now, they were under control. For centuries the people of this center had hunted them, not to kill them, but to make them captives. They were kept in a large, natural rock pit, which had only one opening, and that was closed by a great wooden door. Every year four of the largest ones were caught, tied and carried on carts to the other centers.

The men of this Center had no other responsibility. Naturally, they had become great hunters, fearless men, accustomed to dangers, able to take care of themselves.

When their Old Man received the command to come to the Temple, he called a meeting of the men of the Center.

"I am leaving you," he said simply, "and I may not come back. We have had bad news. The Grain Center on the other side of the Great River has been destroyed. A new kind of man, large as lions and tigers and as many as locusts, came on them, and before they knew what was happening, our people were killed. They sent the news to the Temple and the Old Old Man sent it to the different parts of our land. When these new men or animals or whatever they are move on, they will cross the river and come to our Center. You must meet them, and if you can, you must stop them. At the very first sign of danger, send your women and children to the other centers and you stay here and die. Here is my plan."

The men of every Center were accustomed to obeying orders of the Old Men without question. They could give their opinions if they were asked, but if not asked, they were trained to obey without question or comment. At that time, no one could think of a better plan; so the orders were taken without any discussion. Here is how it was carried out.

At once, activities of every kind started in the Lion Center. Weapons were looked over and repaired. Some men worked from day-dawn to dark, making more arrows. Others headed to observation trees on the east bank of the great river for scout duty. Two of the bravest were assigned the duty of actually crossing the river and making observations concerning the invaders if this was possible. Food was packed in baskets for the use of the women and children, should they be forced to move from their homes. Catapults were placed on the rocks overhanging the gate of the pit where the tigers and lions were kept. The supply of stone ammunition was enlarged. And every day only half a ration of live food was thrown over to the captive beasts who rapidly developed a hunger that made them only more of a terrible threat.

In a week the scouts came back over the great river with a tale to tell that worried even the stoutest hearts. They had seen these strange new men, at a distance it is true, but at the same time near enough to secure some idea concerning them. They were not as thick as grasshoppers, but there were many hundreds of them. They were not as tall as a tiger was long, but they seemed to be, all of them, at least a head taller than the largest of the White Ones. They were nearing the river, and evidently intended to move toward the rising sun as fast as they could travel. There was little evidence of women or children, but perhaps they were in the rear. Even the animals feared them, as all wild life was running away from them.

From the observation trees on the east bank of the great river the scouts saw them cross, floating on dead trees, swimming, on and on. Little judgment, little intelligence, no effort to make boats or rafts, but simply a dominant desire to get across to the other side as fast as they could. Some went under, never to come up alive, but most of them made the trip safely.

With the far distant vision of hereditary hunters, these scouts were able to obtain some details of the new people. Dark skin, thick, heavyset bodies covered with matted hair. Broad, overhanging foreheads, heavy jaws, arms too long for the body. Clubs of wood for weapons. These were the general details as seen at a distance, and in a hurry.

The Lion Center was just two days journey, easy walking, from the bank of the river. The roads through the forest, traveled for generations, were distinct and could be easily followed. The scouts felt that there was no time to be wasted, and they ran as rapidly as possible back to their city. Everything was ready there for instant movement. The women and children started at once on their journey to the eastern Centers, accompanied by the Boy Scouts and their Scout Master as guards. In less than a day the entire beehive was empty. There were, counting the old men, only ninety fighters left, and when they departed from the city it was simply a honeycomb of empty rooms.

To the right of the animal crater rose a lofty pine tree. It was so large and so old that it seemed as though it had always been there. The swiftest runner of the Center was assigned duty in that tree as observer. That left eighty-nine men to fight. Nine men were detailed to act as decoys. That left eighty fighters on the wall of the lion den, hidden in the brush above the great wooden door. As they worked there, preparing the stones and the catapults, one of the old men sighed and died and that left seventy-nine.

Seventy-nine against a thousand, perhaps against two thousand!

Meantime, below them the hungry animals paced restlessly in their prison. Great, beautiful, powerful beasts that knew only two laws, those of the killer and the killed. Now and then two would reach the maximum point of irritation and spring at each other, but mostly they remained separate. They longed for freedom, the lost right to stalk through the forest, through the tall grasses; the right to kill and eat and sleep. Knowing little, they still knew that they were prisoners, deprived of liberty. They resented it.

Down the beaten roads the strangers came like a flood, like a stream of fighting ants. There was little discipline, little intelligence, but still such a combination of fearlessness and brute strength that they would make almost irresistible foes.

Suddenly before them they saw other men, white men, who shot sticks at them, tipped with sharp stones, which passed through their bodies and made them fall, bleeding and dying on the earth road. With cries of rage, the front ranks started to run after these white men; the movement of the entire mass changed from a restless walk to a swift trot. Down through the forest they chased the men who ran before them.

It was autumn, the woods were colored with every tint of golden, brown, purple and green. Through the air the dead leaves showered like a multicolored snow. The white men running ahead were silent; the dark men pursuing them howled and yelped like a pack of hunting dogs after deer.

Suddenly the nine white men came to a ravine, bordered on each side by tall ledges of rock. At the end of the ravine was a gate.

CHAPTER THIRTEEN
The Dark Ones Go Back

TWO weeks later the Old Men were gathered together in conference with the Old Old Man before the altar of the Fire God. They had talked for one whole day. They had listened to the words of Know-More. At the end of the day there seemed nothing more to say, and little more to do. They waited for news from the Lion Center.

In came the messenger from that Center. He was thin and showed the fatigue of constant running. In his right hand he carried a basket of woven reeds; in his left hand his battle ax.

"I have come to make my report," he said slowly.

"You and your words are welcome. But first you must eat. Bring him wheat cakes, and some fresh meat and juice of the grape."

The fifteen Old Men watched him as he ate the food. On the altar the Fire God burned. Except for the crackling of the blazing wood there was no sound. At last the warrior looked up.

"I am ready," he said. "The food was needed."

"Speak!" ordered the Old Old Man. "We are anxious to hear."

"Before Our Old Man left us he gave us his plan for our conduct, and that plan was followed in every way. We prepared the women and children to leave the Center. We sent scouts to the great river. Two of them crossed the river. On the hills above the lion-and-tiger den we prepared for whatever was to come. At last the dark men crossed the river. Nine of our men met them, killed a few with arrows and then ran before them. Thus, the dark ones were led to the mouth of the animal den at the end of the dark ravine. There they turned and started to fight. There were so many of the wild men and they were so anxious to fight that the entire little valley was filled with them. At the right time we raised the door of the pit and the men of our race who were alive ran in, followed by the dark ones.

"Those in front saw the tigers, but they could not go back for the press of those behind them; so they went on. We started to hurl stones at them, with our hands and with the six catapults we had ready. Then, when we saw that most of them were in the trap, we came around and fought those in the rear who were beginning to wonder what the matter was. We shot all of our arrows, and then we fought with spears till they broke, and then we used our battle axes. In the animal-den the lions and tigers were killing and being killed. Those dark men were big and they were strong, and they did not know what it was to be afraid.

"They had nothing but their hands and clubs, made from branches of trees. Afterwards, I found that they did not know the making and use of any of the weapons we had. How they did it, I do not know, but in the end they killed every one of those beasts. I found one man dead, with his body ripped, but he had his great hands around a tiger's throat, and he had killed the beast by keeping him from breathing. So it was a great fight. I and no one else ever saw a greater one.

"Our Old Man had told us that if we could, we must kill them all. And there were just seventy-nine of us to do it. Of course, the animals helped, but when they were all dead and our men were all dead, there were three men still alive of the dark ones.

"So I came down the tree. I was there to watch what they did so I could bring the word to you, but at the same time, I remembered what the Old Man said; so I came down the tree as fast as I could. Two of the dark ones I killed with arrows, and then I went at the last one with my spear. I ran it through him, and he simply broke it off, tore it out of his body and kept on fighting. So I finished him with my battle ax, and here is his head in this basket. I thought you would like to know what they looked like."

He opened the basket, took out the head and handed it to the Old Old Man. He took it in his hands.

"This is an animal," he said simply. "Look at the teeth."

"It is not an animal," countered Know-More. "It is the head of a man. Look at the head bones over the eyes."

"What difference does it make?" asked one of the Old Men. "The messenger says that they are all dead."

"They are," said the messenger briefly.

"Then the nation is safe!" cried another Old Man.

"You speak like a child," cried the Old Old Man. "These fighting men are killed, but what of the females and the children? It is true that in this fight a great number of the dark men were killed, but what of that? Beyond the river are the seeds for another great army of enemies, and what is there back of them? One day I went to the great water, and I saw a tall wave come into the shore, and when it hit the shore, it broke, and that was an end of all that water and all of its strength. But back of it came other waves and still more;

and all day I watched them come and break, and each one carried sand back with it. I knew then that there would be no end to these waves and that, day by day, the sand would be torn away till there would be no more sand.

"And I fear for the White Ones who are few in number. I fear that back of this mass of dark ones there are other masses, just as there were more waves. Perhaps even now they are crowding through the mountains where the sun dies every day, far to the west. They will come on and on, and each wave we will break as we did this one, but in the breaking we will lose the sands of our nation till at last there will be no nation left, and all this country, we love so much, will be run over by these half-men. Our Centers, our knowledge, our books, and clay vessels and stone buildings and all the things it has taken us so many years to learn to make will be torn to pieces and trampled in the dirt by these half men who will not be whole men like we are for many hundreds of years to come."

He turned restlessly in the gold chair and faced Know-More.

"I sent for you days ago and told you of the danger our people faced, and I told you to talk to the wise men and not to sleep day or night, not one of you, till your wisdom showed us how to save our people. What is your answer, Know-More?"

"Nothing. All of our men simply say that nothing like this has ever happened before; so they cannot tell how even to start finding safety. We know a great many things, but how can we know about the things that have never happened?"

The Old Old Man frowned.

"Our Fire God is angry with us. This calamity has been sent as a punishment on our people. Somewhere in our land, the path has not been followed. But I expected better things from you, Know-More. Your talk is the talk of a frightened child. I am not sure of all there is to be done, but of some things I am sure. Messenger! What is your name?"

"Fleet-foot."

"Have you ever departed from the Path?"

"Never."

"Then, obey me. Take this head of the dark one and place it on the Fire God. That is a sacrifice. It represents the kill you helped kill. Now, take your battle ax and kill this man, Know-More, for me, and place him on the Fire God as a second sacrifice. Obey!"

There was no hesitation. The ax swung in air, and before anyone could realize just what was happening, the body of the dead professor had been placed on the head of the dark one.

The Old Old Man stood up and bowed before the altar.

"This is our sacrifice, Mighty Fire God. We give you the head of a dark man and we are sorry we could not bring you all the heads, but the distance was too far, and there was but one man to carry and he was weary. We give you the body of Know-More, who was of all our learned men the most learned, but in our time of distress he became a frightened child, and all of his wisdom did not permit him to help us in our hour of need. So he was useless to our nation, and thus, was an easier sacrifice for us to make, than to give you even our poorest fighting man."

He sat down in the gold chair.

"Old Men," he said sadly, "this has been a great day in our nation. When the record of this day and the story told us by Fleet-foot is written in our skin books, called Histories, our children's children may question just how great our nation really was. Return to your Centers, and try to find an answer to these things. If any are found who have angered our God by departing from the Path, bring him here for a sacrifice. I do not think that there will be any danger for a while, and for a year, maybe two years, the dark people will think twice before they cross the great river. Care for their women and children. Their men were brave men. Of them all, only their Old Man and Fleet-foot live on. But in another spring their Boy Scouts will give us more men. Go back to your Centers and leave me, for I am very tired."

And on the altar the Fire God ate the head of a half-man, part of a race that in thousands of years might become whole men. It also ate the body of Know-More, most learned of his race, the man who knew so much that when he was needed to guide his nation, he could only say that he knew nothing.

CHAPTER FOURTEEN
The Iron Knife

THE Old Old Man was right in everything he had said concerning the immediate future. There were other groups of dark men behind this first group, and they, following in the path of their leaders, swam the river, went down the dirt road and soon came to the place of the battle between the White Ones, the animals and their fellow half-men. What they saw there did not please them, and they went back over the river, and from then on all the dark men went down the country between the great river and the western mountains, but none crossed on the other side. They went farther and farther to the south till at last they came out on another continent, and they spread over that new land, till they, in turn, were wiped off the earth as a child wipes chalk off a blackboard.

In this way they no longer became a source of great danger to the White People and their civilization. The stand made by the men of the Lion Center, the clever plans laid for battle by their Old Man, served the double purpose of temporary protection and future safety. The result would have been different if the invasion had been directed by a higher grade of intelligence, but the psychology of the dark people was not sufficient to cope with the temporary check on their tribal movement; so they slid down the west of the river, and for the time, peace and safety came to all those on the east side.

More Bear and Fire-Man lived on in their cave. They saw no one; thus, knew nothing of the destruction of the Grain Center and the fight of the Lion Men. Rather happily they worked on in the cave, the one learning new ways to harness the breath of the Fire God and have him cook foods in new ways, and the other making repeated experiments with iron, heating and pounding and shaping the metal into shapes that he thought might be useful to his people.

The things he made at first were crude, ugly pieces of metal, not nearly as beautiful or as useful as his weapons of stone, but week by week and month by month, he became more expert, and finally made a knife that would really cut, a hammer that would crush the hardest stones, and what he was really proud of, a metal needle. All through these months of wandering, months of cave-living with Fire-Man, More Bear had never forgotten White Pigeon, the girl he hoped some day to marry. The needle was for her, to sew with, to make the clothing for both of them and maybe for the baby he hoped to have.

"This work with iron is very interesting," he explained to Fire-Man. "Of course, you are more interested in steam, but at night I cannot sleep, because I have so many dreams of just what can be done with hard iron, if it could only be worked like clay or wood. Take our carts for one thing. We can make a cart, and with a great deal of trouble, we can finally make two round things which go around and around and carry the cart. You have seen them, but the wheels break; they wear out. Suppose the wheels were made of iron instead of wood, or had a ring of iron around the wood. Then the wheels would last a long time, and perhaps the cart would go faster. That is just one idea I have. Here is another. When we want to make something big out of wood, we have to take little pieces and bind them together with cords of grapevines or leather. Let me show you something. Here are two pieces of bark. I found two pieces that are soft and thin. I put them together and push this needle through them, and they are bound together. Suppose I had a lot of needles, shorter and heavier than this is, and I should take two pieces of wood and pound those needles through them. I should have one piece of wood instead of two.

"Just that thing means something to me. Do you know what they told me at college? I met a man there, called Know-More. This man says that when our people came across the great water they came on logs, trunks of trees, tied together with leather ropes. I went far down into the hot country, and there came to a fishing Center, and those people were still going out on logs, only they dug the centers out so they could sit in them and push through the water with a flat stick.

"I talked to many of their young men. They took me out on their logs, which they called boats. They showed me the sails. They were all sad, because they wanted bigger boats. They said that if they could only shape pieces of wood and could hold them together in some way, they could make bigger boats and go places in them."

"Why do they want to go places?" asked Fire-Man.

"Because of their hunger for the unknown. You came here, because you had a pain inside you and you wanted to cure you of that pain; even so with these fishermen. They have a great hunger in their heart to see what is far away over the water; yet in the little boats they have, they cannot go far, hardly out of sight of the land. They know of boats and the shape they must be to go fast through the water, and they know of sails. They have even put sails on carts and they make them go on land on long pieces of wood for their roadway. Now, I can give them what they want. Sharp pieces of iron that they can work with to shape pieces of wood, and little sharp pieces of iron that they can drive through the woods to hold them together. Try to see what it means. It means a large boat, large enough for ten people to live in, with much food, and in it these ten people could go to a new land, away from the Fire God and the Old Men."

His voice sank to a whisper.

"That is it. A place where fire could be kept in every home. A place where everyone could eat the food we eat, prepared by the fire; where we could make things of metal to hunt and fight with and to keep warm with in winter time. Then life might be different; just how different I am not sure, and whether it would be better I am not sure, but it would be worth trying. I want to try it, but I do not want to end in the Temple, standing before the Old Old Man to have a spear thrust through my heart and my body placed on the altar to be eaten by this Fire which we know is not a God, but simply a servant of mankind."

Fire-Man looked at him, perhaps a little sadly.

"These are dreams of yours," he said at last, and then, after a long pause, "but of what use are they? You and I know something, but what good is it if we cannot tell the others? Nothing is worthwhile if you cannot tell others. I know a woman who has a pain inside of her like my pain, and perhaps, if she ate this food we eat, her pain would leave her as mine left me, but I cannot go and tell her, for then I should die.

"You worked for weeks to make a little piece of iron to take the place of a bone needle, and you say that you are making it for a woman you want to marry, but you go and give that needle to her and tell her how you made it, and she will see you dead and she will have to go on sewing things with bone and marry a man who uses stones on the end of his arrows instead of iron as your arrows are ended. So we live here, two young men in a cave, and we have to decide between forgetting all we know and going back to the women who love us, or finding new ways of making fire serve us and staying here in the cave alone. What shall we do?"

"I am going to bring White Pigeon here!" shouted More Bear defiantly, as he grasped his spear and stared around into the shadows, as though looking for someone spying on him and listening to every word. "I am going to bring her here, and you bring your woman here and we will start a new Center and a new nation."

CHAPTER FIFTEEN
One More Tiger

THE next morning the hunter and iron worker awoke early. He took the best of his sharp knives and his precious, beautiful iron needle and placed them carefully in his medicine bag with the piece of tiger skin and the tooth of the seacow given him by his father. Then iron tipped arrows and the spear with the sharp metal point at the end and the iron hammer he left with Fire-Man, to whom he said goodbye, promising to return as soon as he could.

The two young men, buoyant with the hopes and dreams of youth, little realized what the future had in store for them. More Bear took a bee-line northward, towards his beloved green-clad. He purposely avoided the Centers. He even refused to talk to the occasional man he met in the forest. He simply gave him the signal of peace and manhood and passed rapidly by him. At last he came to the long river, and up that he went till he came to the gap in the mountain. There he paused. He knew that high above him on the top of the mountain one more tiger waited for the Boy Scouts to start on the path to manhood. He remembered the day when he had faced the tiger with his friends and how some of those friends of his boyhood had been carried to the side of the mountain and thrown down into the trees, hundreds of feet below. One of those boys was the brother of Possert, the Scout Master. He looked up the mountain side and thought he could see, here and there among the green branches of the spruce and hemlock, the white bones of those who had died, trying to gain manhood.

He wanted to think, but his thoughts were twisted. Was it all necessary? What part did the Fire God have in this annual sacrifice of fine young lads? There was the start of the path, and the end of that path was in the Temple, at the Altar of the God. He looked at his left hand, where the end of the little finger had been cut off. That was the blood sacrifice that bound him to the worship of the Fire God. He had taken that God and made a servant of him. He and Fire-Man had used the God; they used his heat and his breath; they had even been able to make him whenever they wanted to. Yet, this was the God that made a nation live in certain ways that were unpleasant and uncomfortable.

And, somehow, the tiger, waiting in the cave up on top of the mountain, was a part of that God. Not the God, but a part of him.

It was springtime. The leaves were budding, the flowers were starting to make the green fields beautiful. Birds were singing, and butterflies were trying their new wings. He wanted White Pigeon, but somehow he knew that there was one more thing to do before he could come to her.

It had been four years since he had been on the top of that mountain. He knew that in a few weeks a troop of Boy Scouts would go there and kill the tiger waiting for them. Some of them would die with the tiger.

He started up the mountain.

At last he came to the cave where the saber tooth animal was waiting for the ceremony that he did not understand any more than the man looking at him understood it. More Bear made his plans. He knew just where he would stand, just how he would stand, just how he would carry out the killing. Then, and only then, he climbed up and pulled on the rope which would loosen the stone and liberate the beast.

He pulled the rope and ran swiftly down into the open space in front of the mouth of the cave. So fast did he move that he was on one knee, his spear in place, one end braced on the ground, the other in the air before the great beast made his first spring.

It was rapid preparation, but it was perfect in its position and time. The hunter knelt on one knee, which was pressed firmly on the ground as did the end of the spear, which was held by both hands. Every muscle was tense. The tiger saw the man and sprang, and as it came down through the air to kill it, fell on the spear, which plunged through its chest and heart. At the same moment that the spear entered the tiger, More Bear jumped to one side and just escaped the killer's claws.

He jumped and he ran. Though, sure of the deadliness of his stroke, he also knew the wonderful vitality of those animals, and that even when dying, they were dangerous. The tiger ran after him, but at every jump was handicapped by the end of the spear's striking the ground and catching in the brush and small trees. He turned to bite and claw at the stick which bothered him, and then he slowly started to die.

More Bear watched him.

At last he ventured near him, and with one swift, vicious stroke, he crushed his skull in between the eyes with his battle ax. Then he pounded and pounded at that massive head till he worked the great canine teeth loose, and these he wiped carefully and placed in his medicine bag. Then, slowly, with the skill of a hunter, aided by his sharp, iron knife, he cut the dead thing up and carried it, a piece at a time, to the edge of the cleft, and threw the pieces over, exactly at the same place where every year some torn Boy Scouts had been hurled. He took dirt and threw over the blood-stained ground, and then, and only then, did he go down the mountain and back to the river.

Plunging into it, he bathed and swam till all the blood was off his white body. He washed the teeth, and he polished them with leaves.

"That was a kill that was worth the killing," he said.

CHAPTER SIXTEEN
The Rivals

ALL that night he slept with peace and many happy dreams, and on the next day he arrived at the Center. Rather quietly he walked into the city and first went to the home of his parents. Many Bear and Lambkin were more than glad to see him. Long ago they had given him up for dead. They sat with him on the bear skins and told him all the news of the last four years. Much of the news was real news to him. He had little to tell of what he had done, simply saying that he had been on the solitary road, trying to learn how things were done in other parts of the nation.

Later on in the day he went to see Possert, the Scout Master. Possert looked at him gravely.

"Where have you been?" he asked.

"Almost everywhere."

"What have you done?"

"Things that needed to be done, and learning the wisdom of those I met."

"Have you heard of the dark people and the battle fought at the Lion Center?"

"Not till today."

"You should have been there. It must have been a great killing, and you would have taken pleasure in it."

"I am tired of killing," answered More Bear, gravely. "I wonder if there is not too much killing? Of course, these dark ones wiped out the Grain Center, and they had to be killed, but it was a price we had to pay, a heavy price we had to pay for that killing. Had we known more, we might have done it in some way without having so many of our men die with the victory. How is everything here?"

"Fine. In a week I start with the new troop of Boy Scouts. You see, I am still Scout Master, and this year we have thirty boys to start on the path to manhood."

"Thirty? A larger number than usual, from what I can remember of the past. Are they good material to make men of?"

"I think so. They have been well trained."

"Hope none of them are killed. Seems a shame to raise boys and then take them down every year and have some killed, just when they are ready to make good men for the Center."

Possert looked at him rather critically.

"But that is the path they must follow. Otherwise, they would never be men. Anyway, there is not much difference in values, having them killed or having them away from the Center, as you have been for so long."

"Perhaps you are right. But I learned a lot during the years I was absent. Nearly all I wanted to know I learned in some way or other. Now, I am on my way. So far, I have not seen White Pigeon. No doubt, she is rather much of a woman by this time."

"She is. More than one of our young men have wanted to marry her. Had you stayed away much longer, you might have lost her. Perhaps you have lost her already. She is so interested in her work with the carrier pigeons that she says she cannot see how she can marry anyone."

"She may tell me that. At least I am going to give her the chance."

"How should you like to go to the mountain with me when I take the Boy Scouts?"

"I think not. You can get along very well without me."

"It seems to me," commented the Scout Master, "that during the four years you have been away something has happened to you. You are not at all the kind of man I thought you were going to be when I trained you as a boy scout. Anything wrong?"

"No. Guess I just became a man. At least, I hope so."

THE young hunter had to go to the pigeon house to find his old sweetheart. He found her busy mating pigeons and making the records. She was so busy that she seemed to have hardly time to answer his greeting.

"I am glad you are back," she said shyly. "In fact, I am very glad to see you, because all of us had made up our minds that you were never going to return. So I went on and kept my days busy with the pigeons, so I should learn to forget you had ever lived. I have done well in my work. In fact, I am in charge of it now, and my pigeons are the fastest in all the Centers. In five more years I think that I shall be asked to train the other Centers in the breeding of fast pigeons. At this time I am very busy. It is the mating season, and we cannot let them mate in any haphazard way. It all has to be supervised."

"I know that, but when can you take a walk with me?"

"Probably in a few weeks."

"How about this afternoon?"

"No."

"Tomorrow afternoon?"

"No."

"When?"

"This afternoon, to have it over with. You see, there is a young man interested."

"I know. His name is More Bear."

"Is that so? I thought his name was Panther?"

"I remember him. Nice enough boy as I recall him. I will see you this afternoon. I am going now."

More Bear hunted up Panther.

"Come with me to the Old Man," he demanded.

"Why? What is wrong?"

"I have a matter for him to decide. It is all according to the Law, and I follow the Path in doing it."

"Then I will go, because we both started on the path at the same time. If it is the Law, I have no choice."

The two young men came into the house of the Old Man. Wrapped in a blanket of racoon skins, he sat on the wall, enjoying the warmth of the sunshine.

"I come for judgment," said More Bear.

"And I come because this man has asked me to, in the name of the Law."

"I will listen to you here," the Old Man said. "As men, you can sit near me and say what you have to say."

"My words come first," said More Bear, in a low voice. "I am a man of this Center. The little finger of my left hand shows that I became full man in the Temple. As a boy, I loved a girl of this Center and she loved me. After I became a man I followed the Lone Journey, as was my right, and I have returned to the Center yesterday. I am ready now to marry the woman I loved as a boy. I am told that during my absence Panther has asked her to marry him, but she refused. As he is still unmarried, it seems that he still wants to marry her. I demand the Mating trial, according to the Law. It is my right."

"What does Panther say?" asked the Old Man.

"More Bear stays away for four years and then comes back and moves swiftly. All he says is true, though I have not told him. But when I became a man I returned to the Center. I have worked for the Center. It is true that I love White Pigeon, but she has not promised to marry me. She says that she will not marry anyone. But if she does marry, she should mate with me, because for these four years I have been a worker in the Center and I love her."

"Yes, she should marry someone," sighed the Old Man. "She should have married long ago."

He looked the young men over carefully. In many ways there was no choice between them. In size, weight, age, and strength they seemed to be well mated.

"Will either of you give way for the other?" he asked.

The only answer he received was silence.

"Then, we shall have to go to the trial. Most of the men are in the Center, so we will have it at high noon. Meet me on the high roof."

CHAPTER SEVENTEEN
The Fight on the Roof

AT noon the Old Man, all the men of the Center, including Panther and More Bear, gathered on the high roof, the place of judgment for many generations. There, decisions were made, council held. A meeting there was always important, a ceremony, demanding the presence of all the men and no women.

The Old Man spoke.

"Two of our men have asked for a trial. They both love the same woman. The best man wins, not the right to marry, but the right to ask the woman to marry. These men are More Bear and Panther. Has any man a question?"

One man spoke.

"Is the trial of blood?"

"It can be. That is for these two men to say. In the old days this trial was always of blood, but for many years no one has demanded it. The Law says that each man can fight with whatever he wishes. Panther, what have you to say?"

"This is a very serious thing to me," replied the young man. "This trial was forced on me, and is not to my liking, but since More Bear has demanded it, I will go on with it. I use my battle ax. This is a trial by blood and to the death. There is no other way."

"What do you say?" said the Old Man, turning to More Bear.

"I do not want any bloodshed," was the reply. "Panther is a brave man and a good man. I knew him as a boy. We were in the same class of Scouts. I like him, but I cannot let him marry my woman. I fight with my hands."

"You have heard these men!" said the ruler. "Has anyone anything to say as to why this trial should not be a blood one, with one using a battle ax, and the other his hands?"

Many Bear stood up.

"One of these men is my only son," he said. "For many months I thought him dead. Now, he has come back to us. It is not my right to tell him what he should do, but I want to say that no one in this Center, or perhaps in any other Center, has ever heard of a trial with one man armed and the other defenseless."

"That is true," said the Old Man, "yet both men act in their right and according to the Law. There are only two things to do. Go ahead with the trial or have them go before the Old Old Man in the Temple at the time of the making of Men and have him decide. If either wishes this, I will so order. Otherwise, the trial will go on as these two men wish it."

"It had better go on," said More Bear. "I am the only son of Many Bear, and I know that he does not want me to come back from the dead and then die at once, but this is a thing of my own, and even he will not stop me in my decision. Let it go on."

"Form the circle," spoke the Old Man sharply. "This is the Law. No one shall go into that circle to aid either man. The trial goes on till one of the men is killed, or unable to fight. Panther and More Bear! Get in your corners, and when I throw dust into the air...start. This is the Law."

The men of the Center lined the low walls of the roof. The sunshine filled the wide open space. The two young men stood in their corners. More Bear with empty hands; Panther with his stone battle ax. The Old Man scooped a little dust from the dirt floor, looked at it carefully and then flung it into the air. A light wind carried it out over the city.

The fighters walked carefully toward each other and then Panther sprang forward, swinging his ax. It was a long jump and a well aimed blow at the head that would have ended the fight at once had it hit. More Bear fell to the floor. For a second it seemed that he had been hit, but in the next second it was apparent that he had fallen as the only way of dodging the blow. He ran back to the side of the ring and then he turned and again faced his opponent who had remained in the center. Again they came together; again the blow was aimed and carried over the fallen body of More Bear. It almost seemed as though Panther was being played with.

For the third time they faced each other. This time instead of a swinging blow, Panther used the overhead chop. But with the ax starting to fall, More Bear threw himself forward and struck Panther at the feet, throwing him forward, but on top. There was a whirling, a vain effort to get a deadly hold, and then they sprang apart, but this time More Bear had the battle ax. It had slipped out of Panther's hands as he fell forward and his opponent had found it first.

He took the ax and handed it to the Old Man.

"Take it," he said. "That also is the Law. From now on we fight my way."

He turned and walked with slow, easy steps toward Panther.

Panther's strength was well known. While not the strong man in the Center he was easily the largest and strongest of all the young men. More Bear was known only from memories of him as a growing boy. The spectators had thought it a most unequal fight when the battle ax had been used. Without the ax they still considered it to be a one-sided conflict with everything favoring the man they were well acquainted with. The thing that pleased them most was their idea that, with the ax out of the way, there would be no chance of a killing.

Suddenly the two men met, each with his arms clasped around the other's body. It was the beginning grip of a wrestling match, a favorite sport with all the men and many of the younger women. It was a test, not only of strength, but of agility, of holds and locks.

The arms tightened.

There was no doubt but that with this hold Panther would slowly crush the other man. Suddenly More Bear changed his grip. One arm went around the neck and the hand of the other arm caught Panther's chin, forcing the head back. Slowly the head was pushed back, back until the stronger man was forced to break his body hold to save his neck. And then came the great surprise.

More Bear picked the other up, held him in the air and started to turn him around and around.

And ended by throwing him on the dirt floor.

He did not follow the advantage but simply stood there and waited till the battle began again. Once more they met, and once again Panther was twirled around in the air and thrown to the floor.

IT was a new form of attack. Something the men of the Center had never seen, something that Panther appeared unable to defend himself against.

It was the novelty of the attack, the simplicity of it, the ease of the execution that deceived the spectators. They only saw what was happening, did not realize the great strength the man was using in the spin, the terrible force with which the dazed Panther was being thrown to the dirt.

But the next time they met, Panther, throwing caution to the wind, plunged in, took his favorite body hold, and held there. His chin down, it seemed impossible to become free from that terrible strangling hold, which looked certain to break More Bear in two. He not only tightened his grip, but he dug his nails into the body to make the grip more certain. More Bear simply stood there, breathing shallowly, his feet braced, and let the other show his full strength.

And that strength was not enough. When the last pound was used, the last ounce of reserve expended, it was not enough. More Bear was suffering, but he was smiling, almost laughing, even though the Panther's claws were digging and ripping into his flanks. It was not till in desperation the Panther started in to bite, that the smile changed to a slight frown. Then and only then did the passive attitude of the challenger change. He raised his dangling arms and placed his left hand on Panther's right shoulder and his right hand around his elbow, and gave one great slow twist.

The older men saw in that twist something of a terrible strength they had rarely seen before, and certainly had not expected to see in this battle. They leaned forward in tense, silent, suspense as they saw that right arm go back, back; saw the right hand loosen and finally drop limp from the elbow, and finally saw Panther jump backward in a last desperate effort to escape the punishing grip.

More Bear let him go, but More Bear was laughing again, the laugh of confidence. With a gesture of sheer supremacy, he waited a few seconds and then, in one jump, caught his prey and once again raised him for the fatal spinning throw. Panther was thrown to the floor, once, twice, three times, and the last time he lay there, unable to rise. There was not a mark on him, but More Bear was covered with blood from the bites in his shoulder and the nail gouges in his sides.

He turned to the Old Man.

"Is it enough?" he asked. "I do not want to kill. This man is a brave man and of value to the Center. He is helpless. I do not want to hurt him."

The Old Man took a handful of dust and tossed it in the air. Once again the golden particle drifted in the spring wind, each little piece made more golden by the warm sunshine. At last the air was clear and still Panther remained unconscious, asleep, stunned by his repeated falls.

"It is enough," said the Old Man. "This is the end of the trial. More Bear has done wisely in not going on to the killing. Has anyone a reason why this matter should not be ended?"

No one had an answer.

More Bear walked over to his prostrate foe, bent over him and started to move his arms. At last Panther opened his eyes.

"He is not hurt," said More Bear. "In a little while he will be all right. I did not want to hurt him, but it was very necessary that this thing happen. Now, I will go."

He was the first of all the men to leave the high roof. Looking neither to right nor left, speaking to no man, he left the Center and went directly to the lake, where he swam in the cold water till all the blood was washed from his white skin.

CHAPTER EIGHTEEN
White Pigeon is Stolen

HE came out of the water, stood in the sunshine till he was dry, and then, with his blanket of skins wrapped around him and his medicine bag in his hands, he sat down on a heavy clump of moss and shut his eyes.

During the long, lonely months with Fire-Man he had learned to think. Now he was doing this, and his thinking was not at all peaceful.

"I am on a new trail," he said to himself. "Few of us have ever been this way, and of those that have, only Fire-Man and I are alive to tell it. We have lost all we had, our God, our families, our homes. Nothing remains to us of the old things. We have left the Path and the new way seems to be one of strangeness and doubt. I should never have come back to my home, because it is no longer mine, and the ways of my people are no longer my ways. Even today the men wanted Panther to win, because they knew all about him and they knew nothing of me. Even the way I fought was new to them. White Pigeon would have been better off had she stayed with her pets and married the Panther. He would have made her a good man, while I will bring to her nothing but trouble and sorrow. If I knew where and what a real God was, I would ask Him to help me, but the only God I know of I have destroyed. The old Path is ended. It would be best to stay here till I find a new Path I can follow."

All that day and all that night he stayed there by the lake. The next morning his mother, Lambkin, came with corn cakes and a bowl of milk. He did not speak to her, and she placed the food by him, sat for a while and then returned to the Center. More Bear left the food untouched.

Late that afternoon the Old Man and Many Bear came to the lake side. They were clad in their best robes.

They sat down beside the silent young man.

It was not till a long time had passed that the Old Man spoke: "We come to tell you something that you must be told. Will you hear us?"

"I hear you."

"Panther has gone from the Center, and he took White Pigeon with him. It happened last night. It seems that the woman had gone to look after her birds and he caught her. There was a struggle; she did not go willingly. At least, we are sure he used force. Some of the cages were broken; there was blood on the floor."

More Bear frowned, but he did not make any comment.

"The trial should have settled this," went on the Old Man, "and in doing the thing he did, Panther has broken the Law. Your father and I have come to you to tell you. If you wish me to, I will have all the men of the Center take up the trail. So far, all we know is that Panther went towards the river."

"The Old Man and I have talked this thing over," said Many Bear, "and we do not think this is your own matter to decide. The Law is the Law, and it should be settled by the entire Center. But we can only say that to you, and allow you to say your say."

More Bear threw his skin blanket off his shoulders and reached over for the bowl of milk and the cakes. He ate the food slowly, folded the blanket, and handed it to his father. Bending over, he carefully tightened the leather laces of his shoes. Then he took his weapons, his spear, bow and arrows, hunting knife and battle ax and handed them to the Old Man.

Only then did he break his silence.

"What has to be done in this matter," he said. "I will do by myself. You speak of the Law. I know the Law. Possert taught me all of it when I was a Scout. The Law says that after a trial, if the man who loses departs from the decision, he shall die. The Law also says that if a man takes an unmarried woman into the woods against her will, he shall die. Perhaps I should have killed Panther when he was asleep, so he would never have done this thing. But he has done it, and now there is no undoing. I will not have him trailed like a wild thing by our hunters. What has to be done I will do by myself, and alone."

Many Bear shook his head.

"You cannot go into the woods without weapons..."

More Bear tied up the leather thongs that held his medicine bag to his belt.

"Thus I go. Ask the Old Man. He will tell you that thus men go at times."

"He is right," answered the Old Man. "At times, when great things happen to a man, so he does not think clearly but seems to have his body filled with an unseen thing like a God, he goes into the woods without weapons, and stays there, and because even the animals see that he is no longer a real man but filled with a God, they do not harm him. There is something strange and different with your son, Many Bear, but he has a right to do everything he speaks of, and no one has a right to say 'No' to him. Now, I will tell you one thing. Our hunters followed this man to the river and then down the river. They tracked the trail to the lone pine tree on this side of the Water Gap. You will be able to pick up the trail there. Can we get food for you?"

"No. I have eaten. And now I am on my way, Father. I want you to tell Mother that I thank her for bringing me the milk and the corn cakes, and tell her also that till this thing is done that has to be done, I will not eat again. I wish that you had more sons, for I fear that the only one you have has caused you more sorrow than happiness. And now I go."

He started off on a dog trot, which, by dark, would bring him to the lone pine tree. There he would have to stay till daybreak, and from there pick out the trail.

The two older men watched him.

"He is my son," said Many Bear. "He is my son and the son of my wife Lambkin. All the time she was carrying him she was making a book. She said that her child would be a strong male child, but she did not want him to grow up to be a hunter. But after he came, she did not try to train him in her ways. But she did teach him to read the books she had made. Do you suppose that what she hoped for and what she did made the young man different from other young men?"

"I do not know," answered the Old Man. "I remember you when you were a Scout. I was your Scout Master. You wanted to be different. After you had become a man, nothing would content you but that you must go to the Tiger country and kill one alone without help. There was a time when you came back that you were different. It was not till you married and had a child that you were like the other young men. Your son has been away for many moons, and we do not know what he did or what he learned or what he thought. I watched him when he fought Panther and for a while it seemed to me that he did not care, that nothing made any difference. It was not till Panther bit him on the shoulder that he started in to fight, really fight. Even when he won, he did not want to kill, and after it was over he came here by the lake and went into a dream instead of claiming White Pigeon. Something is wrong."

CHAPTER NINETEEN
Panther is Killed

TWO days later Scout Master Possert left the Center, with thirty Boy Scouts, to start them on the road to manhood. They marched down the river road. There they met, as they had met for many years, the Scouts from the other three centers of that part of the nation.

Possert came back, with thirty Scouts, a day earlier than usual.

He at once went to see the Old Man.

"You are back soon," was the comment.

"I am. I have a most peculiar tale to tell."

"Tell it…"

"I took the troop of Boy Scouts down to the Water Gap as we have done for many years. The other three Scout Masters met me. We saw the man who feeds the tiger. He said that he had thrown into the feeding hole a large calf seven days before, according to his custom. The tiger was there at that time. At least, he heard him roar when the calf dropped into the hole. At the appointed time the Scouts were placed in their proper place and we loosened the stone; so it rolled away. We had told the Scouts to shoot the arrows at once at the hole, and thus we hoped to save their lives. We felt that every year there had been too many of the boys killed. They did as we commanded, and we killed the animal that jumped out. But it was Panther who died with thirty arrows in him instead of the tiger. And that was something that seemed very strange to all of us. He was dead, so he could not tell us anything about it. But it seemed to us that since he had been in there he must have killed the tiger. So

183

we went in, and there was no tiger and no signs of any tiger and no signs of any fight. Now, Panther might have gone in there to escape More Bear's anger and the tiger might have escaped, but if he did, how did Panther shut the stone behind him after he was alone in the cave? For you know that the stone can only be moved from the outside.

"We have carried the body of Panther back with us. The arrows were left in him. He came out fighting. Perhaps he thought the men of the Center were waiting there to kill him, and while he was wrong in many ways, he was not a coward. Here is another thing that I cannot understand. He had all his weapons with him when he died, and there were no wounds on him except those from the arrows."

The Old Man frowned.

"White Pigeon came back to the Center yesterday and she was alone. Perhaps she can tell what happened. I will send for her and talk to her alone."

The young woman came at the orders of the Old Man. She was in her ceremonial dress as fitted the occasion, and in her hand she carried one of her pets.

"My Child," said the Ruler, "I want you to tell me freely the things that have happened to you. I want you to tell me everything, and leave nothing unsaid."

"I will do that," answered the woman. "After the trial, about which I only heard a part, I went, as always, late in the evening to see my birds. There Panther caught me, tied me and carried me off on his shoulder. Far from the Center he put me down and made me walk with him. He told me that he would kill me if I did not come. He said that he was going to take me into the dark forest and live there always with me, and the way he talked I knew that he was a bad man. We reached the lone pine and from there went over the mountains into a country I had never seen before. Every time we stopped, he tied me to a tree. I left a trail, a broken twig here, a kicked pebble there, and now and then a hair from my head. I knew that someone would follow us. The second day, when I was tied and Panther was resting, More Bear came and they fought. Panther had all his weapons and More Bear had nothing but his hands, but in the end Panther was down and tied with the very leather thong with which I had been tied, then More Bear took up Panther on his back and told me to follow. We went to the mountain above the Water Gap, and More Bear dropped Panther down a hole in the rocks, and then he sat there and asked me to marry him.

"He said that he did not want to live in the Hunting Center. He was tired of killing all the time. It was hard for me to understand just what he wanted to do, but it all amounted to wanting to marry me and go away somewhere and live with him. It meant that I had to leave the pigeons, and in the end I told him that I could not leave them. I was willing to marry him, because I loved him, and always have loved him, but the breeding of the pigeons was my work. He thought a while about it and then said that he would see me safe to the Center and then leave on another lone journey.

"That is all I know of it. He left Panther in that hole with all of his weapons. He brought me safely back and left me at the lake. Then he left me and went away without a blanket and without any weapons, not even a knife. Simply his medicine bag tied to his belt. It seemed to me that he was very tired, and some of the things he said made me feel that his Spirit had gone out of him. But one thing I am sure of. He did not hurt Panther. There were some corn cakes left in Panther's bag, and he threw them down the hole so the man would not be hungry."

"Was More Bear hurt?"

"Yes. An arrow went through his shoulder, but he said it would heal."

"In all of this, my Child, you have done just what you could do. Both of these men were in love with you, and you are in love with your pigeons. Go and forget both of them, and in a year marry. That is my command. In a year marry, and perhaps you can do this and at the same time take care of your birds. You can go."

The Old Man sent for Possert.

"We will go to the Temple as usual," he said. "I will send word to the other three Old Men. Our boys have not followed the Path, but this was not through any fault of theirs, and perhaps when the Old Old Man hears the story, he will allow them to be made men even though they killed only a Panther instead of the tiger. It may be that some change will have to be made anyway, because the Lion Center is no more, and all of the hunters are dead. How can we get tigers every year? But all this is strange to me, and I am following new paths that I cannot understand. What happened to the tiger? There is no doubt that More Bear took Panther and placed him in the deep hole where the calves are placed to feed the tiger. The stone was not moved and yet the tiger was gone. What is your idea?"

"A simple one. More Bear did not want to kill Panther. He would not have put him down there, knowing the tiger was there to kill him. He knew that the Scouts would be there soon to start on their way to manhood. He knew that Panther would live till we opened the door, I am not sure that he thought the man would be killed, but he did know we would find him and bring him back to the Center to punish him for breaking the Law. He did not want to have a part in that punishment. All he wanted was to save White Pigeon. Evidently, he and your daughter could not agree about marriage. I have been talking to her. She would not leave her pigeons and he would not stay here in the Center. So he brought her back to you and your wife. Your wife works with glowworms, your daughter with pigeons. The ways of women are past my understanding. It seems that any woman would have been glad to mate with More Bear, but your daughter wanted to go on with the breeding of birds instead of with the breeding of children. Did More Bear kill the tiger?"

"I do not know. But I do know that Many Bear killed one by himself when he was a young man. It may have been in the breed. But if he did, he did it knowing that without the tiger our boys could not start on the Path."

"And none of them would die. Remember that. Your brother and More Bear were close together. Like two leaves on the same branch. He saw your brother killed. He saw the other boys killed. And several times he has said that he wants no more killing. In the trial he refused to kill Panther. When the man took your daughter and there was a fight, he again held his hand from the killing. I know what I think. You had better go now and prepare for the journey to the Temple. The wisdom of the Old Old Man will have to be great to tell us just what the Path is from now on. But I am glad that your daughter, White Pigeon, has come back to you and to your wife and that she is not harmed."

Possert returned to his home. "Why did you send your man away?" he asked his daughter. "I thought that you loved him?"

"I love him more than any man," the young woman answered, "but he wanted me to leave my pigeons."

CHAPTER TWENTY
Fire-Man is Captured

AFTER More Bear was satisfied that White Pigeon was safe, he started off into the forest. He was sure that there would be a number of sharp questions asked him if he returned to the Hunting Center, especially after Panther was found in the tiger cave. In spite of the added responsibility, he would have been glad to have taken White Pigeon with him, but he realized that there was a good deal of common sense in her refusal to leave the Center and that he did not have very much to offer her.

Under his worry was a great homesickness for the little cave he and Fire-Man had lived in for so many months, and he did feel sure that if he could only spend some more months there, some of his problems would be solved. So with the sure instinct of the trained woodsman, he took a bee line for the cave and his friend. He ate as he went—roots of shrubs, fresh berries, an occasional rabbit or squirrel, killed by a thrown stone. Avoiding as best he could the danger of the larger carnivora, he came, at the end of six days of almost constant travel, to the cave that had been a real home to him.

Fire-Man was gone.

Everything in the cave was broken, destroyed, strewn in a hopeless wreck over the floor.

There was only one answer to the question.

His friend had been discovered, made a captive and even now was being taken to the Temple for judgment and death.

He carefully searched through the broken things on the floor and finally found what he was looking for, the flints they had used in building fires. He placed two of the best of these in his medicine bag and then went outside the cave, and sat down.

To his great surprise, a young woman stole out of the bushes and called to him.

"Are you More Bear?"

"I am. Peace be with you. Who are you?"

"I am Little Rabbit. After you left this place the man you called Fire-Man came to his Center and talked to me. We have known each other for many years, since we were little children. He asked me to come and live with him, and though I knew that he had done a bad thing, I did as he asked me, because I loved him. I kept warm by his fire and ate the food he made for me in that fire and the thing was bad, but the food was good. Early this morning I went out to pick berries, and while I was gone, the men came and took my man and broke everything he had made, and I suppose they would have taken me if they had found me. He told me about you, told me how you looked, and when I saw you and the way you acted, I was sure you were his friend."

"This happened this morning?"

"Yes, only a little while ago."

The man started to examine the tracks in the dirt. At last he said, "There were only a few men. Have you food?"

"Just these berries."

"We will eat them and then we will get Fire-Man, because if he reaches the Temple, he will die, and that must not be, now that he made the Fire God a servant and tamed a woman. Let us eat and go. The track is plain. The men think they will not be followed and have taken no care to hide it."

Traveling fast, they came on very fresh tracks by late afternoon.

"We must go slowly now till dark. Then these men will tie Fire-Man and sleep till morning. They will take little care, because they do not fear you and do not know about me. Then we will get Fire-Man and we will go toward the setting sun and over the great river. The dark ones are there, but I am not so much afraid of them as I am of my own people."

It was the time of the full moon. There were great shadowed spaces in the dark forest, but here and there were open places, which were almost as light as day. More Bear took his treasured iron knife out of his medicine bag and carefully rubbed the edge with a small piece of sandstone. He and the woman were on a ledge of rock. Below them, and not far away, Fire-Man sat on the ground, his back to a small tree and tied. Three men sat before him in the moonlight.

"You wait here," the hunter told the woman. "We will be back soon."

From far away the three men heard the hunting call of the saber tooth tiger. Once heard, it could not be forgotten. Again the beast screamed, and this time it was nearer. They jumped to their feet, spears, bows and arrows, battle axes ready to defend themselves as once again the cry came, still nearer.

And then between them came a fighting, slashing thing that raked them with knife-like claws, all the time howling its rage, and then as suddenly left them in a great silent fear.

Not one of them was killed or disabled, but all of them had on their bodies the long marks of the tiger's claws. And when they had time to think about him they found their prisoner gone.

They arrived at the Temple just as the meeting of the Old Men and the initiates was taking place.

"We have a tale to tell," their leader told the Old Old Man.

CHAPTER TWENTY-ONE
The Old Old Man Worries

THERE was a young woman in our Center, called Little Rabbit. She was not a large woman, and she spent most of her time making food, and she did not want to marry. Many days ago she left the Center, and as she was alone, and we feared harm would come to her, our Old Man told me and two others to track her and bring her back. We followed her tracks and found that there were two, and at last we came to a cave where we found the man, but the woman was away and the man told us that she was dead and there was no need to look for her.

"This man said his name was Fire-Man. He would not tell us what his name had been or what Center he had come from. But in the cave were many things which showed that he had departed from the Path and had broken the Law and should be brought to the Temple and judged by you.

"The Law that he broke was the Law of our Fire God. He had the God in his cave and he boasted that he had made it, kept it for his servant, used the breath of our God.

"We went a day's journey and then rested for the night, and he was bound to a tree. Early in the night we heard the cry of a tiger and soon we were attacked. All of us were hurt, but none killed. The tiger, however, carried our prisoner away with him. We left at once and we traveled all that night, it being moonlight, and we have come here to tell the tale."

"You did not examine the ground for tracks."

"No. We left at once before the beast returned to kill."

"He came among you, slashed you all and yet did not kill?"

"He did not kill, except the prisoner we were bringing here."

"My son, Many Bear, is here. He has hunted the tiger. I will ask him to look at your wounds."

Many Bear came from his group of men and carefully examined the three men. Their cuts were from one to two feet long, with clean edges, and were already beginning to heal. At last he told them to put on their blankets.

"What do you think?" asked the Old Old Man.

"I have hunted the Tiger. Once I killed one by myself. I have seen the bodies of many men and boys killed by these beasts. These cuts were not made by a tiger's claw. Had they been, these men would not be here today. They were made by a knife."

"What kind of a knife?"

"Not by any kind I know of. Certainly not by a stone knife."

The Old Old Man opened his medicine bag and took out a knife.

"When I first became the Ruler and came to sit in a gold chair, a young man was brought here, charged with breaking the Law, and he told that he took our Fire God and iron ore and made sharp things with it, and he had this knife that he made. I placed the knife in my Medicine Bag and there it has been since. Take it and tell me whether with such a knife a man could have cut these men the way they were cut..."

Many Bear took the knife, felt the edge, made sweeping movements through the air, and then handed it back to the Ruler.

"Such a knife would do it."

"Perhaps such a knife did it!" cried one of the Old Men.

"No. The man who made this knife, burned on the altar long ago."

"That is true," agreed the Old Old Man, "but this breaker of Law called Fire-Man was taken by another man and not by a tiger, and that other man had an iron knife with a sharp edge to it."

Many Bear went back to his group, frowning.

CHAPTER TWENTY-TWO
Gods of the Dark Ones

IN the meantime, Fire-Man, More Bear and Little Rabbit were going to the land of the setting sun. "And what we find there is something we can only tell when we get there," remarked More Bear. "All I know is that it is death for us to stay in the land of our own people, and it may be death to leave our own land, but between these endings, I think that the last one is the better of the two; so we will go. First, I want to go to the Lion Center. There was a great fight there, and since that fight no one has ventured that far toward the great river. There will be weapons there, arrows and spears and battle axes, and we must have something to fight with. Otherwise, we shall be like little animals in the jaw of a lion."

"We shall be anyway," replied Fire-Man. "I am little and I never have fought much, and though you are strong, you are but one."

"We will go and get weapons as soon as we can. There is no time to make any. But in the meantime we shall be safe at night."

"How can we be safe at night without a cave?" asked the woman.

"Climb a tree," replied More Bear. "Be like the little monkeys that I saw in the hot country. They are little and cannot fight, but no lion could get to them. We will live on in some way. But we will not live with our people, for all of us have left the Path and broken the Law, and anyone has a right to kill us."

For ten days they went toward the great river, and finally they came to the deserted Lion Center. The buildings had not been harmed in any way. They went to the place of the fight, and there they saw hundreds of white bones, picked clean by the birds and washed by the rains and snows and whitened by the summer sun.

"This was a great fight," mused the hunter. "I heard of it from my father, Many Bear. The men of the dark people came here, and on one side they faced the lions and tigers and on the other side the men of the Center slew them, and there they all died. Only one man was left to carry the news to the Old Old Man. There are good weapons here. We will each take a bow and arrows, and Fire-Man and I will pick out spears and battle axes, if we can find some that have not been broken. These strangers must be very great in size. You can easily tell their head bones from those of our race. We will spend the night in a room of the Center and then we will go to the Great River and in some way cross it."

"How shall we do that?" asked Fire-Man. "They say that it is very large, and now it is in the spring flood."

"We will again do as the monkey folk do: find a dead tree and, sitting on it, we will go where we go. If we had time, we would make a boat, but for all we know the hunters are after us. We can only be safe when we are across the water."

They did just the thing that the hunter suggested. They found a dead tree, washed down by the flood and held to the bank by the roots. By digging the dirt away, they loosened it so that it started to float down stream, and on it they rode all that day and all the next night till the morning brought them to the other side. It was mud and swamp and little bugs there, but the hill land was beyond, and afternoon brought them to the mountains and forests.

"I wish we could find a cave," sighed Little Rabbit. "A cave and something to eat besides the berries."

"We will get everything in time," said Fire-Man, cheerfully, "and we will have fire, and food cooked by it, and we will keep warm."

"And I will go and kill meat, and if there is iron ore, I will make tools and a needle for you so you can sew skins. What is to be will be, and we shall not know of it till it happens to us, but anything is better than to be tried in the Temple and killed and burned on the altar of a Fire God that we know is simply our slave. But first let us hunt for a cave and some dry wood and I will make fire, and we will eat, for there are many birds and little things here, and the killing of them will be easy, for they are many and do not seem to be afraid."

They did not find a cave, but they did find a flat rock up on the side of the mountain, with high rocks back of it and steep rocks filling many feet on the sides and front, so that it could be defended easily. There they carried branches of trees and dry bark, and Fire-Man took the flints and cleverly started a fire and soon he and the woman felt better. The hunter left and came back in a little while with a large bird which they cooked in the fire. The woman had the only blanket of fur, but with the fire, they did not need it. So they simply spread it on the rock and slept on it.

Often during the night the hunter put more wood on the fire.

From the mountain above them and below them some of the dark people saw the fire. When morning broke, many more came to see it, so that soon from every tree and from every high rock they looked on the White Ones around the fire.

More Bear was the first to see the strangers. He told the others.

"This is not a time of fighting. These people are on the trees like so many leaves. We must simply stay here and wait to see what they will do."

In an hour they saw two men approach the rocks twenty feet below their fire, carrying a dead deer. This they put on the rocks and ran away.

"They want to feed us!" exclaimed Little Rabbit.

"Either that or they want to trap us, and this is the bait," argued Fire-Man.

"We will wait and see," decided the hunter.

All that day the inhabitants brought things for the three on the rock; they brought furs and nuts and even a live goat with a kid.

"I am going down there and will take their gifts," whispered More Bear. "I think they are trying to make friends with us. I will carry a burning branch in my hand and go down among them, and if they kill me now, it will be nothing more than they could have done earlier."

So with a fire brand in his hand, he climbed down the rocks. He put on one of the skins, ate some nuts, cut a leg off the deer and then climbed up to the fire. A murmur came from the forest, a murmur of almost happy satisfaction.

It was Fire-Man who arrived at the right solution. "They think the fire is a God," he shouted, "and, because we made it and have it serve us, they think we are greater Gods. We came into their land, and they feared that we would destroy them; so they brought us gifts to ease our anger. Now that we have taken our gifts, they are no longer afraid.

"They are trying to tell us that they are glad. They are simple folk, though great in bone and muscle, and we are to them Gods. We can be their Gods. They will worship us and care for us and serve us, as our people have served the Fire for so many generations. If we live with them, they will be our people, and we will be their Gods. Thus, we can live safely and in peace, for they seem to be a mighty people."

"I believe you are right," replied More Bear. "Let us go down among them, each carrying the fire, and we will let them carry us to their Center where we will live and rule them."

"I can see some of them among the rocks," commented the woman, "and they certainly seem to be more like animals than men. Do you think they will kill us when we go down?"

"We shall have to see," replied Fire-Man. "One thing is certain. If they want to kill us, they can do it, no matter where we are, because they are many in number and we are but three. So we might as well do as More Bear suggests: go down to them as though we were not afraid. Perhaps, if we carry the fire with us, they will fear us so that they will not hurt us."

Slowly, the three climbed down the rock, each with his weapons and each with a fire brand in his right hand. Once on a level, they were surrounded by a ring of hundreds of the strangers who kept, however, at a respectful distance. They were large, powerful, brute-like men, with no women or children. In their hands they carried clubs of wood. They were covered with hair, and though they walked upright, their thick bodies and long arms, heavy frontal bones and deep-set eyes gave them indeed an appearance of huge bears or gigantic apes. A few of them wore skins, tied to their shoulders, but most of them were without anything resembling clothing. Their speech was simply a low chorus of harsh murmurs, but a few of the leaders seemed able to command, by sharp barking noises, the beginnings of a real language.

More Bear placed his weapons on the ground, handed his fire brand to the woman, and started to walk towards them with his arms in the air his palms towards them. It was a gesture of peace. They seemed to understand it, for one of the largest of the men came to meet him, holding his hands in the same position, but soon falling to the ground, a token of surrender. The hunter went up to him, patted him on the head, and taking his hand, raised him to his feet, and then patted him on the shoulder. Taking off his own fur robe, he traded it for the lion skin worn by the leader of the dark people.

It was a symbol of friendship, of offered peace that was well understood. The dark man turned and faced his people and uttered a long series of barking sounds. At once, the dull murmur of fear changed into a chorus of loud, laughing sounds. They seemed to be happy. More Bear took the leader and led him over to Fire-Man and the woman. Once again he took the blazing branch in his hand, and pointing to his mouth, showed that they wanted food and water.

The tall dark leader pointed to the land of the setting sun and showed, by signs, that they should walk there. The hunter showed that they would not walk, but must be carried.

Thus, in a little while, the three adventurers were being taken on the shoulders of the beast men through the forest, but each of them held tightly to his precious fire brands.

In a little time they came to the village of the dark ones. There were huts, crudely built of sticks, leaves and mud. There, were the women and children. In the center was a large hut, evidently the home of the big man of the tribe. He offered it to the three strangers. More Bear refused to take it; but selecting an open space, he took his lance and drew a large circle in the dirt. In the middle of the circle were placed the three blazing sticks. He showed by signs that they should bring him more dry wood, and this he placed in a pile outside the circle. Then they placed their weapons and their furs inside the circle, built a larger fire, and sat down. Food was brought them; meat, nuts, and fruit. Around them the dark people squatted, chattering noisily. The leader passed around, showing everyone his new fur, which added greatly to his importance.

CHAPTER TWENTY-THREE
A New Life Begins

"THESE are simple people," commented More Bear to his companions. "They are very simple. They know nothing of the things that we know, and because we know so much and because we have fire, which they have never seen before, they think that we are Gods and will worship us, even as we worshiped the Fire God before we knew that it was not a God but a servant.

"So we will live here and be Gods. Thus we can live and be safe. We will teach them some of the things we know, such as making weapons of stone, and the use of the bow and arrow. We will teach them to fight and how to wear clothing and live in better houses. First, we will make them build a large house for us, and in that house we will have an altar, and there we will keep the fire, and we will have no one feed that fire but ourselves, and we will not let them use the fire, for then they would think that they also were Gods and as wonderful as we are. Then they would kill us and take our places. As long as we can teach them things they do not know and make them feel that we are great ones, they will care for us."

"And they will not kill us?" asked Little Rabbit.

"No. I will not let them," said Fire-Man, bravely. "You are my woman, and I will care for you. I wonder if there is any white clay around here? It would be fine to build things like I had in the cave. There are a lot of things I want to do, and now that there is no need to fear, I can do them in a bigger way. Perhaps I can find new ways to use this fire and its breath, the thing I call steam."

"And I will work with iron when I have the time," cried More Bear. "But first I must teach them how to make fighting things out of stone and how to use them, and we will then have a great army of fighting men. When others come against us, we will drive them away. We will build a city with walls to it. They are big men and very strong, and they can build a city of stone. Thus, we will live, no matter who comes to destroy us."

"But where will you get a woman?" asked Little Rabbit.

"I only want one woman," was the reply, "and she wants her pigeons more than she does me; so for the time till she learns more wisdom concerning what a woman needs, I will live without any of her sex, for I certainly cannot mate with one of these women."

Both of the men were exceptional personalities, but Fire-Man had little of the leader in his makeup. It was necessary for More Bear to make all the contacts with the new race. This he did in a surprisingly capable manner. He took one man and taught him to flake stone for making spear heads and how to fasten spear heads to a stick with leather thongs. He drove this man to his work and did not stop until he not only was able to make spears, but was also capable of teaching others. In a month every man in the tribe had a spear, not a beautiful one, but at least a useful one. Then he taught the tribe to use the weapons in fighting and hunting, how to throw them and how to thrust with them. The men learned quickly, in fact, showed a remarkable degree of ability for acquiring the new knowledge.

From a tribe of shiftless, aimless half men, the strangers rapidly grew into a community of workers. Not all were willing to learn the new ways, but when they found how much easier it was to hunt with spears than with sticks, they became enthusiastic. They were taught how to make war clubs, and finally a few of the brighter ones were told about the bow and arrow and were taught how to use them.

MORE BEAR learned their language, a rather easy thing to do, as they did not have more than twenty sounds for the most common things, and no nouns. Once this language was learned, it was easier to command the people. With this ability, work went ahead faster. A large hut was built of rocks, and in it the new Gods lived with their fire. A twelve foot wall of rocks and earth rose around the village. Everybody worked. Keeping them busy was a simple matter after several of the shirkers were killed. By the time fall came, a walled city stood in place of the former collection of one-room huts. Everybody wore some kind of fur. All the men had stone weapons and knew how to use them. Hunting was easier, food was more plentiful. Nuts and grain and dried meats were collected and stored against the needs of the winter.

"They are children," commented More Bear, "but in this childhood of theirs, there is promise of a new and a great race. They learn easily. Their Chief now knows some words of our language. I have let him be a great man, and as the great man, he tells his people the advantage of living with Gods. So far, all is well with us, and the time may come when we shall see the wisdom of what we have tried to do."

The time came that very winter. It was a cold winter, and other tribes of the dark people were restless and hungry and on the march. They came in a great mass from the land of the setting sun, and found the city of the new Gods in their path. Under the old life it would have been a conflict of beast against beast, with the stronger and the most numerous killing the weaker. But this time they found the weaker on top of a wall and able to kill them with flying sticks and to crush them with stone hammers and pierce them with lances, and at the head of the defenders, three white ones, carrying long sticks in their hands. These were red on top, with something there that they had never seen before. Therefore, they feared so greatly that the many fled before the few and the city was saved. And then the dark ones knew, indeed, that their Gods were great Gods, and they worshiped them as never before, because their tribe had been saved from destruction.

After that battle a very peculiar thing happened. Just what caused it, what primitive thought was back of it, the three Gods did not know, but after it happened they worried a great deal about it, wondering what it meant and how it could be kept from happening again.

Five of the leading men of the dark people asked to come into the Temple and to bring gifts to the Gods who lived there. Before that, they had all been allowed to visit the Temple, and see the fire burning on the altar. A very few of the leaders had even been allowed to eat meat cooked on the altar, but that was a very special reward of great merit.

These five men were permitted to enter the Temple, and they brought with them one of the young girls of the tribe. According to the standards of beauty of the dark ones, she was very lovely. She was dressed in fine furs. Each of the men brought a branch of dry wood, carefully cut to fit the altar.

That ceremony also was a thing that had been taught them. The food of the fire had to be of the best, and everyone who visited the Temple had to bring a piece of wood with him especially cut and carved. The visit of the men, their bringing of the wood, was understood by the three Gods. It was a part of the new Law. What they did not understand was the reason for the woman's being brought into the Temple.

CHAPTER TWENTY-FOUR
A Gift to the Gods

THE whole trouble arose over a lack of language-communication. More Bear knew all the language of the dark ones, and the Chief of the tribe knew about twenty words of the new Gods. Two of the words that he and almost all the people knew were *gift* and *God*. The word, *Fire,* had not been taught to them. It had been thought best to make them feel that the name was too terrible for them to say and that the saying of it would kill them.

The Chief and his people had an idea in their heads. They wanted to make a real gift to the three new Gods and the wonderful nameless thing that lived on the stone altar. So they brought this young girl into the Temple, and after placing their gift of wood on the fire, they sat down, and the Chief started to talk. As best he could, using few words and many signs, he told about what the Gods had done for his people, how they had taught them about the use of stone for weapons and how to kill at a distance and how to save food and destroy their enemies. And because of this he and his people wanted to make a gift to the Gods. Would the three Gods accept the gift?

"I know what they want to do," exclaimed Little Rabbit. "They think that More Bear is lonely, and they bring this girl here to mate with him and work for him as his woman. I know the girl, and have taught her how to make fur into clothing and how to make corn cakes. She is a nice girl, perhaps the best of all that have not been mated."

"That must be it," agreed Fire-Man. "And they think that if she lives with More Bear, and has children by him, it will keep us here because the thing they are afraid of is that we will leave them, and never come back. Better take her, More Bear."

"No!" said the hunter. "I do not want her for my woman, but she could live here in the Temple and work for Little Rabbit and learn many things, and then she could go and teach those things to the other women, and the tribe would be better. I think I will tell these men that their three Gods will accept this gift."

He stood up and talked to the five men. As best he could, he told them that the gift was acceptable to their new Gods and that they might leave the girl in the Temple. The acceptance seemed to make the five very happy. They crept over and kissed the feet of the three white ones, and then they went over to the girl. But before they could be stopped, before the three had any idea of what was going to happen, they drove a spear through her breast and placed her bleeding body on the fire, and then placed new wood around it.

The three Gods saw it all, but too late to do anything more than watch it. Then the five left, happy, and shouting, to tell their people that the Gods had taken the gift, thus showing that they were still going to remain with them and help them.

Alone in the Temple, the three sat silent.

At last More Bear whispered, "We did not understand them. It was a sacrifice to the Fire and not to us. The thing that we hated in our own people, human sacrifice to a Fire God, who we learned was not a God at all, has happened here, and unless we do something to stop it, it will happen again and again. Once the Old Old Man told me to kill one who had wandered from the Path, and I did so, and watched his body as it was placed on the Altar of our old God in our Old Temple, and I knew then that it was an evil thing to kill. Since then I have never killed except to protect myself or feed myself with the meat of animals.

"We came here because we were sick of the Path and wanted to find a new way for men and women to live. And even though these dark people were almost beasts, we thought we could teach them a new and a better way. We taught them part of what we knew; all they could learn. We saved them from the famine of winter and the terror of the other tribes, and this is the result! They love us; they fear us; they worship us; and because they want to show us how they feel, they bring us a young girl and kill her as a present to us. We were simple to think that they wanted me to mate with her.

"How could they think that I, as a God, would mate with one of their women?"

"We are but three, and they are many," cried Little Rabbit. "Tomorrow, or the day after, sometime they will bring another girl to burn on the altar, and there is only one way to save her, and you know the way."

"It is not a pleasant way, but you are right. They learn a thing slowly, but once learned, they will not forget. We will take off our clothes and cover our bodies with mud, and we will sit in the open place of the city, and we will not eat or talk; thus, they will know their Gods are angry."

FOR three days the Gods did this, rising only to go into the Temple to attend to the fire. The dark ones brought the best of food, the finest skins; they sat around the three in a great circle and mourned in a low wailing chorus. On the fourth day the three went to the river, washed, put on their best skins, ate in the presence of all the people and went back to live in the Temple.

And all the tribe rejoiced, starting in with their usual work, and there was feasting and happiness in every hut.

The next day the five great men of the city came again, bringing with them another girl. She was the daughter of the Chief, his treasure, and worth much in his eyes. She was dressed in beautiful skins. Her hair was combed as Little Rabbit had taught the women to comb it, and around her head was a gold ring, brought from some far corner of the earth. Her body was not very hairy and she had been washed just as the people had seen their Gods wash.

The Chief made his talk. He knew why the Gods were angry with the people. It was because they had brought a common girl to give to them instead of the daughter of their Chief. Now, they were doing this. Would the three Gods take the gift?

Fire-Man and Little Rabbit looked at More Bear anxiously. How would he act? Was it to be another living sacrifice?

The hunter stood up. A great man by this time, almost as tall as the tallest of the dark ones. He cried to Little Rabbit to bring him a corn cake and a piece of dry meat. Then he went over to the six worshipers, and told the five men to sit down. He took off his tiger skin, and laid it on the ground. From the girl's shoulders he removed the deer skin and laid it on the ground and then he wrapped her in his tiger skin, and on his shoulders tied the deer skin. He took off her gold band and placed it on his head. He broke the corn cake and gave her half and told her to eat. He tore the meat, and told her to eat, and as she ate, he ate. Then he took the girl over and had her sit by Little Rabbit.

It was the mating ceremony. He had often watched it. Now he turned to the five men.

"This is my woman," he said. "The Gods accept your gift."

CHAPTER TWENTY-FIVE
Children in the Temple

WHEN the news of the event was spread through the tribe, there was great feasting. Life had been different for the dark ones since the three Gods came; yet, always there had been the lurking fear that someday the Gods would leave them. Now, that the best beloved one had taken the daughter of the Chief to be his woman, to mate with her, perhaps they would remain; perhaps they would never leave them. It was a wonderful thing to have happen.

The girl herself thought it wonderful. To be the woman of such a man, with such a beautiful white skin; to be the woman of a man who knew so much, who had come to them with that burning thing that was on the Altar; to mate with a God and bear children to him; why, it was just too wonderful to be true. She knew when she had been taken into the Temple that she was taken there to be a sacrifice, but instead of death, a husband waited for her, and what a husband!

"It is not at all what I expected out of life," explained More Bear to Fire-Man and Little Rabbit, "but perhaps it is the best thing to do. We cannot go back to our people except by the path of war and killing. We shall have to live here till we take the last journey. So I will mate with this woman, and you, Little Rabbit, will have to teach her the ways of the women of the old race, and perhaps as the years pass, I shall be able to forget White Pigeon and the love I had for her. Perhaps this woman will live to comfort me, and bear my children, for all she knows is how to mate with a man and work for him. The things, such as painting pictures, making books and mating carrier pigeons are arts that she cares nothing for."

"This is a good thing you did," commented Fire-Man. "What will you call her?"

"Her own name is Sun Head," was the hunter's answer, "because, of all the girls in the tribe, she alone had a golden band to wear on her head. So even though she is dark, I will call her Sunshine, for there is a gleam to the ring she wears when the sun shines on it. She will live with us and care for Little Rabbit when she bears your child, Fire-Man, and soon she will have a child of her own, perhaps many, if she is like the other women of her race; and then we shall need a larger Temple, with more rooms in it. It may be that we shall live to see the children of our children rule this race. They will be half gods, but there will be no more killing, and from now on only fruit and grain will be brought to burn on the Altar."

More Bear's prophecy turned out to be true. In a month Little Rabbit gave birth to a daughter, but never again did she have a child. Sunshine presented her husband with a son every year for five years. They were all great, sturdy children, who were almost white, and had larger heads than the heads of the other children. During those five years there was peace, but the winters constantly grew colder. Other tribes of the dark ones drifted before the cold towards the hot lands, but the tribe of the White Gods simply built warmer huts and prepared more food for the winter time. Still, there was no fire except in the Temple, where the Gods and their families lived.

Ten more years passed, each with a colder winter and a drearier summer. Fire-Man's daughter was fifteen years old. More Bear's youngest son was nine. The girl was little and frail, but the five boys were great, wonderful lads, with the sturdy body inherited from their mother and the keen intellect of their father.

And then came the great killing.

CHAPTER TWENTY-SIX
The Gods Move On

PERHAPS it was the relentless cold; perhaps the wet, sunless summers. A new disease may have drifted on the bitter winds from the west. Whatever the cause, the dark people of the city began to die.

They died fast. So quickly did the pestilence pass from hut to hut, from family to family, that soon there were none left to take the dead out of the city. Death came to the Temple. First, Little Rabbit died, and then her daughter, and then Sunshine, and last of all Fire-Man, always frail, followed them. Spring came finally; the snow started to melt, and a few of the hardier trees dared to start budding.

More Bear walked through the city that had been his home for so many years, and found that it was a city of the Dead. No one was left except his five sons and himself.

The boys followed him, wondering what it all meant. The oldest was almost a man, taller than his father, while the youngest was a sturdy lad, almost able to take care of himself under any circumstances. They walked through the city, found out the terrible truth and then went back to the Temple and to the fire. It was then that More Bear told his sons the decision he had made.

"We are going to leave here and return to my people. There is no use remaining here, for if we do we also shall die sometime soon. We will take food with us, and our weapons, and we will leave. I will take nothing else except the gold band your mother, Sunshine, wore the day I mated with her. What the new Path will be I do not know, but I do know that we have come to the end of the old one. All I know I have tried to teach you. Except that you are darker and larger, you would pass for boys of the white race. You are my sons, and I am your father, and we will stay together on this new Path, no matter where it leads. I think that my old people have suffered from cold and hunger and have died, even as my new people died; so we will go to the old Temple and see what has happened to them."

"Shall we cross the great river and see the dead city of the Lion Center and all the other wonderful things that you have told us of?" asked the oldest son, who had been called First Man the day of his birth by his proud father.

"We will. We will even go into the Temple. The last time I was there the Old Old Man was Cellar, my father's father. Perhaps he is dead now, and another Old Man sits in the gold chair I have talked to you about."

"A real gold chair?" asked the youngest boy.

"All gold. You know what gold is. I have told you that the head band that your mother wore was of gold metal. This chair the Ruler of my people sits in is of the same metal and nothing else. Hammered gold, because they do not know of iron, heated in the fire and shaped as I have taught you to shape it. We use fire as a servant, but they think it is a God."

"Tell us again about our Mother and how you mated with her," said one of the boys.

So the father told them about Sunshine, and how he had saved her from death, and how she had been a fine woman and a good mother to them, and they sorrowed as they heard the tale, for all of them loved her, because of the many things they remembered of her.

The next day they started on their long journey through a land that was dying from the cold. Each night they built a fire to warm themselves and cook their food and keep off the wild things, made desperate by the cold and hunger.

At last, they came to the Temple. There, were gathered the last of the White Ones.

Cellar, the Old Old Man, still lived on his gold chair. He was indeed an old man by this time; too old, he thought. In the Temple with him were five men, seven women and their children three, four boys, old enough to become men, and one woman who had never married. There was still some wood remaining of the great pile that used to be kept as food for the Fire God. There was still a little food. Around the Altar of the Fire God there was a little space of warm air, beyond that, all was cold. It was May, but already the snow of another winter was beginning to fall.

Twenty-one people in the Temple, all that were left of a once great people.

More Bear, in the prime of his manhood, and his five sons walked into the temple. When they saw the people there, they were filled with a great wonder, and a great pity.

The hunter walked up to the Old Old Man.

"I am your grandson, More Bear," he said, "and these are my sons. My people are all dead, and I have returned to the place of my beginning."

"You have come to die with us?" asked the Old Old Man.

"No, to teach you how to live. Here are just a handful of people, but there are children here, and men and women who should bear more children. What are you doing to save them? To keep them well and strong so that they can be like the lone pines and start a new forest, a new people?"

The Old Old Man looked at him and in that look there was doubt.

"Where have you been, More Bear? We have not seen or heard of you for many years. I heard words that told me you had not followed the Path."

"Those were true words. I found the Path you taught me was false. I lived with a man, called Fire-Man, and together we learned that your Fire God was not God at all, but that he should be used as a servant for our people. We learned to use him to warm ourselves and to cook our food and to make our weapons and our tools. His breath we called steam and put it to work, grinding our grain. When your people took Fire-Man and were bringing him to the Temple to kill, I saved him, and with his woman, Little Rabbit, we went beyond the great river. There we lived with the dark ones and built a city. We were Gods there, and the fire was just our slave.

"I mated there with a fine woman. These men I bring with me are my sons. Now, all my people are dead, and I have come back to this Temple to find only a few of all the race I knew of as a boy and young man.

"They are cold and sick, and they also will die if you do not save them. They need to be near the fire. They need food, cooked in it. If they have it, they may live. Give the order for them to come closer to the fire. Make it larger. I have meat with me, and I will show you how to put it in the fire that you may eat it and live. You are the Old Old Man. Give the order and save your people…"

"I will give the order that you shall be killed," the Ruler said. "While I am the Old Old Man, no one shall boast of leaving the Path and live to boast again. Men of our race, kill this man, for he must die and burn on our God."

The five men moved, hesitated and stopped.

More Bear laughed.

"They know I am right and that you are wrong. The old Path is gone, and no one will follow it, because it was a wrong Path. Give the order and save your people!"

The Old Old Man stood up. In his hand was a stone knife.

"I will kill you myself!" he cried, and tottered forward.

More Bear made no effort to save himself, but his son, First Man, sprang forward, and just in time drove an iron tipped spear into the breast of the Old Old Man.

"I had to do it, Father," he shouted. "I did not want to do it, but I had to. You would have let him kill you."

"You did well. There was no other way."

He walked up to the gold chair and sat down in it.

"I am now the Old Old Man," he cried. "Obey my orders, or my sons will slay you as they slew the other. Bring wood and build a fire. All of you come here and warm yourself by it. Those of you who can, bring more wood. I will show you how to put meat in the fire and how to bake your corn cakes. My sons and bring in fresh meat, so all may eat and live. This fire that you have so long worshiped will now be only your servant. It is not a God, but just something we can use and live by. Go and get earth and fill the cracks between the stones. Work, eat, keep warm. Bring those little children near the fire. Get their cold bodies warm. Feed them with this meat that I will show you how to cook. The Old Path is gone. The old Fire God is dead. I am the ruler, and I will save you if you listen to me. Otherwise, you will all die, and you shall take this fire off the altar and build many little fires, so that you can gather around them and live, because you will be warm."

They obeyed him. They took the meat and put it in the fire as he showed them, and for the first time in their lives they ate cooked meat. They put the corn cakes in the ashes and ate that, and with warm food in their bodies and the glow of the many fires warming the Temple, a new hope came into their souls.

CHAPTER TWENTY-SEVEN
The New Path

MORE BEAR decided that it was impossible to winter in the Temple; so he led his people to the hot lands. He taught them how to make fire every night. But as they fled before the cold, the winter followed them. At last they came to the end of the land, and while it was warm there, with sun shining and flowers blooming, he did not feel safe.

"We could live here," he told his sons, "but perhaps only for a few years, and then we should die from the cold. We must go on. When we left the Temple, there were twenty of the White Ones with us. Now there are but ten—and seven of them are women and little ones. We must get to a warm country, where it will be warm always."

"But where can we go, Father?" asked First Man. "For all sides of us have nothing but the water, and above us is the cold land that we came from."

"We will build a ship," answered the hunter. "A ship is a house of wood that can travel on the water. Cut down trees and start making nails of iron as I have taught you. Start the women sewing furs together so that they may make things to catch the wind that will make the ship go. Have the little children gather nuts and grain and have one of the men kill deer and dry it over the fire. We will make pots of clay for holding water. When all is ready, we will get in this ship and go to a warm land. There we will start a new race, journeying on a new Path. Make everyone work. There is no time to be lost."

For a year everyone worked. At the end of that time the little band had a ship large enough for the few that still lived.

It was a crude vessel, but a wonderful one, considering that no one who helped build it had ever seen such a ship before. Yet, it floated. It had a mast and one large sail, and in the ship there was room for all and enough food to last several months.

When everything was ready, More Bear called the people together. There were just fifteen other than himself.

"Here is the new Path," he told them. "I and my sons are going to get in this ship and go over the water to find a place where it is warm so we can live. Of you, there are three men, and seven women and children. There is room for all, and I want you to come, but if you do not want to do so you shall stay here and live or die as you wish. I will not order anyone to come with us, but there is food enough and room enough for all. Come or stay as you wish, but I and my sons are going this afternoon."

Two men and their women refused to go, but asked that their children be taken. More Bear was willing to take them.

So the passengers of the boat included the Ruler, his five sons, one man and his woman, three little children, all girls, and a middle-aged woman, who had never married; in all, twelve persons. Slowly, they pushed the boat out into the deep water and raised the sail, made of skins. The wind from the west caught it, filled it and started the boat towards the place of the rising sun.

More Bear stood at the end of the ship, holding the long oar, which served as a rudder. The others, except the children, started to prepare the evening meal.

The woman, who had never married, walked up to More Bear. In her left hand she carried a little basket, covered with skins.

More Bear looked at her, but did not speak.

"We are going a new way, More Bear," the woman said. "Now that we have started and the old life is past us, and is dead, as our old race is, will you speak to me?"

"I will, White Pigeon," he replied. "Years ago I would have mated with you, but you would not go on a new path. Now, we are on a long journey, and all that has happened in the past seems like a dream that has left nothing but memories. But one thing I would say. Years ago I loved you and wanted you for my woman, and during all the years I have never forgotten you, and I have never ceased to love you. Till now, I have not spoken to you, because I was minded to make you do the first of the talking."

"And now I have talked. I do not know where we are going or what land we shall come to, but I want to say this. I have always loved you. I wanted you to carry me off with you the day that you rescued me from the Panther, but you said I should decide for myself, and no woman can do that when she is in love. So I left you, because you would not force me to go with you. But if you will have me now for your woman, I will be your wife .for the little time we have left, and I shall be glad to be your wife, More Bear."

The hunter called to his son, "First Man! Bring me the gold band your mother wore."

The young man brought it and More Bear put it on White Pigeon's head.

"From now on you are my woman, and I am going to call you Sunshine, for that is a good name for you, and you will wear this gold head band, and when we come to a warm shore and start a new race, you will be the wife of the Ruler of that race, and what you say I will do, because I have always loved you," And he kissed her.

She seemed very happy as she stood beside him.

Suddenly he said to her, "What have you in the basket?"

"Two of my best pigeons. I have cared for them tenderly for three years. They are a little old, but when we have a chance, I think I can raise more. We will want carrier pigeons in the new land. Don't you think so, More Bear?"

"Certainly. We shall have to have pigeons," he replied with a smile.

THE END